THE ESSENTIAL HEIR

MAREE MANDERS

CHAPTER 1

*T*he constant beeps from the heart rate monitor fill the hospital room around you, you focus on your grandmother who is laying in the bed in front of you. Since your parents were tragically killed in a car crash 15 years ago, this lady has been your lifeline. She took you and your older brother Jasper in and raised you both single handedly, all the while carrying on a successful fashion house. As you try to focus on your grandmother, the thoughts enter your mind that just an hour ago, you were both in her office discussing the upcoming fashion show and then she grabbed her chest and collapsed in front of you.

As you sit there, wiping tears from your eyes, the doctor enters the room, "Hello, Miss McIntyre."

"Hello doctor, is she going to be alright?"

"We have run multiple tests, I will be honest with you, it is not good news, your grandmother suffered a serious heart attack, she is in critical condition, the next 24 hours are critical to her survival".

"Oh no" you respond as you squeeze her hand.

"I am sorry I do not have better news for you, she is as comfortable as possible at the moment, you are welcome to sit with her as long as you want to, rest assured, we are doing all we can to bring your grandmother back to you."

"Thank you doctor, I appreciate everything you are doing?

"Ok, I will leave you two alone now."

"Thank you"

As the doctor leaves your squeeze your grandmother's hand, "Hey Grandma, it is me Tori, you will be fine, hang in there darling, I am not going anywhere," tears stream down your face.

As you sit there, stroking your grandmother's hand, memories flood your mind. You recall how she collected you and Jasper from school they day your parents died, took you home and although, struggling with her own grief, gently broke the news to you both. She allowed both you and Jasper to travel through all the stages of grief and stood by you supporting you both the whole time. She helped you prepare for your first school dance, your first school play, taught you to drive and was there cheering you on when you graduated high school and business college years later. Your tears turn into smiles at all the wonderful times you have shared.

As you sit there reminiscing, all of a sudden, the machines in the room start beeping loudly and staff are rushing in from every direction.

You stand to the side, in shock, "What is happening?" you scream.

A nurse turns to you, "I am sorry, your grandmother appears to be experiencing another heart attack, I will need you to wait outside please, while we attend to her," you can sense the panic in the nurse's voice, you reluctantly step aside and watch helplessly as the medical staff attend to your grandmother.

As you wait outside, you try to call your brother Jasper again, unfortunately you have not seen him in many years, since he moved away to follow his acting career. You have both lost touch as you have both been busy building your careers, but you know he should be made aware of the situation. The call goes to voice mail again, fighting back tears you leave a message, "Jasper, it is Tori, Grandma is gravely ill, she is St Peters hospital, please come as soon you can or at least return my call please." Just as you hang up, the doctor appears before you with a dishevelled look, " Miss McIntyre , I am deeply sorry, your grandmother suffered another heart attack and we tried desperately to save her, but unfortunately she has passed.", the doctor reaches for you, but you step back in shock and cry out, " No, there must be something you can do, please" tears stream down your face.

"I am deeply sorry, but there was nothing more we could do" the doctor replies, "Is there anyone we can call for you?"

Shaking your head, you lift your hands to your face, "No, there isn't anyone I need right now, I just need to see her please."

"Of course, take your time."

You make your way slowly into the hospital room and see your grandmother resting peacefully. You grab her hand and all the tears from the day release again as you sit with her.

As you finally decide to leave, your phone rings, it is Jasper, you break the news to him, and he agrees to return home to help with the arrangements for the funeral.

A week later and the day of the funeral has arrived, all the preparations have come together, and you make your way inside the funeral chapel. Jasper returned a couple of days ago, and although he helped with the plans, things are still a little strained between you both, as it has been quite a while since the two of you were together.

Your fellow work colleagues arrive and embrace you and offer their condolences again. Your grandmother was not only an inspiration to you but has been a role model and mentor for many staff members.

The funeral service flows without any problems and there are many wonderful and humorous memories shared of your grandmother. As the service concludes and your grandmother is laid to rest next to her beloved partner and your grandfather who passed away just a year before your parents, you are happy with the day and feel content that she would have approved.

Jasper heads back to Los Angeles the next day as he has an important audition scheduled.

CHAPTER 2

*I*t has been 3 weeks since the funeral and you arrive at the lawyer's office, the day has arrived to read the will. You make your way inside and are directed to the boardroom to meet the lawyer. Jasper is unable to make it in person but will join via a video conference.

Your lawyer, Dean arrives, "Hi Tori, how are you going?" he asks.

"Hi Dean, yeah I am doing ok thanks" you respond.

Jasper dials in, "Hi Dean and Tori, Sorry but I don't have a lot of time, can we get started?"

"Sure, no problem, it shouldn't take long, as you both are the only living relatives of your late grandmother, we are here to read the final will of Esther June McIntyre" continues Dean.

Feelings of grief threaten to overtake you again and you try to hold back tears, however you look at screen and Jasper appears emotionless, you notice him constantly checking his watch.

Dean continues to read the will, "McIntyre fashions will continue to transfer 25% of monthly profits to Jasper Brent McIntyre, Jasper and Tori will agree to divide my belongings between themselves. I hereby leave my primary residence to Tori, Now we come to the matter of McIntyre Fashions. I advise that I intend to pass sole ownership to Tori, on the proviso that she safely produces a biological heir within 12 months from the date of reading this well. Should Tori be unable to produce an heir, within this period, then it is my intention for McIntyre Fashions to be jointly inherited by both Tori and Jasper."

You cannot believe what you have heard, in order to remain in control of the company you have worked in since finishing college, you must have a baby as an heir. How could she put this requirement on you? You gasp in shock, "Dean, this is crazy, Grandma is telling me that in order to keep this business that I have spent the last 5 years working in and building with her, I have to have a baby within 12 months, is that right?"

Dean looks at you and responds, "Yes Tori, that appears to be what your grandmother has directed."

You shake your head in disbelief, how could she impose this on you, you turn to the screen and see Jasper, he is smiling as he comes to the realisation that McIntyre Fashions could soon become partly his. Disbelief begins to turn to anger, Jasper has shown no interest in this company, he moved away as soon as he finished college, and rarely returned for visits, and had minimal communication with you or your grandmother.

Dean continues, "Well that is it for the reading of the will, I will provide you both with copies for your records, I understand that this is perhaps not what you expected Tori, but it is what it is, your grandmother was very insistent that McIntyre Fashions stay within the family and have a clear line of succession."

"Thank you, Dean, I look forward to receiving the copy" says Jasper, with a sly smile. "I have to go, I have a filming session to get to, nice to see you again Tori, Bye."

"Yeah Bye, Jasper" you manage to say, as you fight back tears.

As soon as Jasper signs off, you look at Dean, "Grandma's requirement is absurd, Is there anything I can do to contest this?"

"Unfortunately, not Tori, your grandmother was in sound mind when she made this will and I managed this update personally, so I assure you it was managed correctly and legally."

"Ok, I am just blown away by this, I know you would have managed this legally, I just need time process this and think what I am going to do" you manage a smile at Dean, you get up and shake his hand and turn to leave. "Thank you, Dean."

"No problem, Tori, I will take care of the necessary steps, if you need anything further, please let me know" says Dean.

As you make your way to your car, the tears you have been holding back break through and you sit sobbing in your car for what seems like 15 minutes. Once you recover, you make your way to your best friend Lexie, you have a regular catch-up dinner planned.

A short drive later, you arrive at Lexie's door and taking a deep breath you ring the doorbell. Lexie opens up the door, "Hey lovely, so great to see you, come in" she says as she pulls you in for a hug.

In Lexie's arms, you break down again.

"Oh god, Tori what is going on?" Lexie asks as she quickly closes the door and leads you into the lounge.

As you sit down, you turn to her "Lexie, it is unbelievable, I have just come from the reading of Grandma's will, and she has required that for me to keep McIntyre Fashions I have to produce an heir within the next 12 months".

Lexie laughs, "What? Are you serious? that is ridiculous."

"I know, but that is what she wants, otherwise the business will be shared by myself and Jasper, I can't believe that Grandma would do this to me, how the hell am I going to have a baby in 12 months, I don't even have a boyfriend, I can't believe Jasper will get half of this company, he has done nothing for this company, he left us, I am so angry".

"I know Tori, it is bizarre, I will get us a drink, dinner is just about ready, we will sort this out."

You follow Tori to the kitchen, help her serve dinner and then sit and begin to work out how this can be sorted.

As you both sit down to eat, Lexie asks "So have I got this right, your grandma has stipulated that you must produce an heir within 12 months to gain full ownership of McIntyre Fashions?"

Reluctantly, you look at Lexie "Yes Lexie, that is what she has directed, according to the solicitor Dean, it has something to do with securing succession for the business, or something like that."

"Wow, that is pretty major, have you given any thought as to how to satisfy this requirement?"

"Well, it is going to be pretty darn hard without a partner right now, isn't it? So, I guess I might have to get used to sharing the business with Jasper?"

Lexie pauses for a moment and then continues, "Not necessarily Tori, there may be a way to satisfy this requirement and stop Jasper pushing into the company."

You look at Lexie with a puzzled look "What are you suggesting?"

"Have you thought of using a sperm donor? that will fix the problem of not having a partner, and you will be satisfying the requirement of a biological heir for your grandma, she didn't state you had to be in a relationship with someone to have the baby, did she?"

You think for a moment and then reply "Well no, Dean did not mention that requirement, only that I had to have a baby, an heir. Ooh that is an idea, but it is a bit creepy and clinical though don't you think?"

"Yeah, I know what you are thinking Tori, but what other choice do you have, you have been so busy with the business, you haven't been on a date in years, and it is the only solution I can see that will satisfy the requirement within the deadline."

"Oh Lexie, I don't know, it is all very creepy as I said, I have to think about it, it is all so hard" you respond as you slump back in the chair after finishing dinner.

"Yes, think about it, it might be the only chance you have to keep Jasper out of the business that you and your grandma worked so hard on, so what else was in the will?"

"Well, grandma has left me the house, and Jasper and I are to split all her belongings as we see fit, and she has agreed to continue letting Jasper receive 25% of monthly profits".

"Oh wow, you get the house, which is wonderful, bet Jasper was not happy?" asks Lexie cheekily.

"No, I don't think he was until he heard about the baby requirement, then he couldn't help hide the smile on his face" you say as you shudder with the memory.

You spend the next few hours catching up before the events of the day begin to catch up with you and you decide to head home and catch some sleep.

CHAPTER 3

*T*wo weeks later you are sitting in the waiting room at the local sperm donor clinic, awaiting your appointment with the specialist to discuss your options. As you flick through the brochures, too nervous to fully take in the literature, your name is called, and you make you way into the consulting room.

"Good morning, Tori, pleased to meet you, my name is Stacey, and I will be assisting you on your journey to be a mum," Stacey says with a smile.

"Hi Stacey, thanks for meeting with me, I am here to discuss my options" you reply nervously.

"Great, ok let's get started, tell me why you have made the choice to have a baby with a sperm donor?" asks Stacey.

"Well, Stacey, I will be honest this may sound odd, my late grandmother, in her will, placed a requirement on me that in order for me to inherit the business I have worked so hard in since graduating school, is to have a baby as an heir to the business."

"Oh, I see, that is different, but we can work with that, I must ask though having a baby is a big commitment, how do you really feel about being a mum?" Stacey asks.

You sit for a moment, and then "Well Stacey, I have always wanted children, I lost my own mother at a young age, Grandma took my brother and I in and raised us both, we were extremely close, but I always missed my Mum and want to have a close relationship with my own children. I just thought, I would have more time, and that I would have a partner at least."

"Ok, well you have come to the right place here, we can make your dreams of becoming a mum come true."

"Sounds great, how does it work?" you ask.

"Of course, let me explain, you will need to set up your profile account online, answering a series of questions to allow us to accurately match you with a selection of potential donors. After an initial non-refundable payment of $500 a list of the potential donors will be sent to you to review, Once you have selected your preferred donor, advise us and we will begin the insemination process by which we will harvest your eggs, fertilise them in our lab and then arrange for the transfer to take place. This stage will cost an additional $4,500. I must advise you although we are very experienced in the fertilisation process, that there is no guarantee that the transfer will be successful, so please bear this in mind." Stacey explains.

"Ok, sounds fairly straightforward, thank you" you respond.

"Good, I will begin the setup process of your online profile and email you the link to make your initial payment and begin the profile set up process, keep an eye on your email for the link, I will also hand you this information folder for you to review which has a lot of information about the process and frequently asked questions. If you have any additional questions, please let me know and I will be happy to help you," says Stacey as she hands you the information pack.

"Thanks Stacey, I will have a good read of this pack and be in touch if I need any clarification."

"Great, thanks for coming in Tori, I look forward to working with you to achieve your dream of motherhood" smiles Stacey.

"Ok, thanks Stacey, I appreciate your help" you respond as you stand up, shake Stacey's hand and make your way to the door.

As you drive back to the office, your mind is full of all the information you discussed with Stacey, it is going to be a very costly process and there is no guarantee of success. However, if you want to keep Jasper out of taking joint ownership of McIntyre fashions, you will have to try this sperm donor option. After arriving back at McIntyre fashions, you make your way to your office and check you emails and find the profile setup email from Stacey. After paying the initial deposit amount, you begin completing the necessary application questions and reviewing the information pack. While reviewing the frequently asked questions, you are relieved to discover that the sperm donor will have no claim on the baby and your details will remain completely confidential to the chosen donor. Also, the only information on the sperm donor you will receive will be a photo and any health history information. Their personal details such as name and address remain confidential. As you continue to read the information pack, an email comes in, and based on your profile set up questions, there is a list of potential donors already for your review. As you review the email there is approximately thirty potential donors to review, you are overwhelmed as you begin looking at each one. There are several possibilities, based on the profiles that are provided, the entire process is so overwhelming, and you begin to get a headache, you happen to look up and see fashion designer Evan walk past your office. Evan Thomas has been with McIntyre Fashions for the past year, and has proven to be a wonderful asset, adding a fresh flair to the business. All of sudden an idea enters your head, "Could I ask him to be my sperm donor?" It seems quite a bold proposal, but you know Evan, he is a reliable caring person, with great values, not to mention he is very handsome and athletic, all the qualities you would want passed on to your future child. You sit and ponder this idea for a while, and you begin to pace around your office trying to find the courage to talk to Evan. Before you can stop yourself, you open your office door and head to Evan's office. Nervously, you knock on his door and enter. Evan looks up, "Hi Tori, how are you?" Evan asks.

"Hi Evan, I am good, can I see you in my office for a minute?"

"Of course," Evan responds as he gets up from his desk and follows you to your office.

Once in your office, you close the door, and begin to pace nervously, "Evan, I have an important matter I would like to discuss with you, I do not expect an answer straight away. As you know, my Grandma has just passed away," you glance at Evan, and he nods at you. "A couple of weeks ago I met with her lawyer for the reading of her will, Grandma has decided to pass ownership of the company to me."

"That is great news Tori, congratulations, but what does that have to do with me?" asks Evan.

You take a deep breath and avoid Evan's sight "I am getting to that; it is a bit delicate."

"Ok, I am listening, go ahead" says Evan.

"Unfortunately, Grandma placed a condition on me inheriting the business" you continue pacing, "She has stipulated that for me to inherit the company, I need to give birth to a baby, an heir, within the next 12 months otherwise my estranged brother Jasper will stand to inherit joint ownership".

"Oh wow, that is unusual" Evan says.

"Yes, it was quite a shock to me when I heard this requirement. Evan, as you may or may not be aware I am not currently in a relationship so I would like to ask if you would be willing to help me to have a baby, by donating your sperm?" Evan's eyes widen and he falls back into his seat. You continue "Evan I am overly impressed with your work here, your creative flair is second to none, I would like to offer you your own fashion line, with full creative freedom, if you would agree to help me to have a baby,"

Evan appears speechless, he finally is able to compose himself enough to speak. "Tori, wow, I don't know what to say, this is not at all what I was expecting you to ask me" he runs his hand through his hair and exhales deeply.

"Evan, I understand this is a major request, if you agree, it can all be taken care of via a sperm clinic, where you could leave your deposit, which will then be used to fertilise my eggs which the clinic will harvest from me. So, it will all be very confidential and clinical." As you continue to pace, you glance at Evan, and you can see him deep in thought.

"Evan, I really need your help, I will be able to take care of the baby on my own, I don't expect anything from you to raise the baby, please think about it, you will be really helping me so much."

You turn to Evan, he looks up at you, "Tori, this is massive, I really need time to think about it."

"Of course, Evan, I understand, take what time you need, but I don't mean to pressure you, but I will need an answer soon, as plans need to be made soon as it will take time to organise and there is no guarantee of success on the first cycle."

Evan rises to his feet, and looks at you, "Yes of course Tori, I understand, I will get back to you as soon as I can, is there anything else? Can I leave now, I have a lot to process"?

"Of course, Evan, that is all, thanks for hearing me out," you head to the door and Evan follows you.

"Thanks Tori, I will get back to work now" Evan says as he leaves.

Your eyes follow him as he returns to his office Evan sits down and you can see that he is still shell shocked, feelings of guilt begin to engulf you, you ask yourself "What did I just do? Look at Evan, he is in complete shock, How could I have asked that of him?"

As you make your way back to your desk, you try to focus on your tasks, but can't help watching Evan, like you he is trying hard to focus, but you can see that his mind is a million miles away, as he blinks hard to try to focus on his designs, making adjustments and then quickly erasing them.

You decide to review the potential donor profiles again in case your plan with Evan fails you will have a backup. Eventually you narrow down a shortlist.

As you begin to pack up for the day and head home, you are about to leave your office when you look up to see Evan heading for the elevator. You decide to hold back and wait for Evan to leave first feelings of guilt and nerves over your earlier conversation overtake you and you do not want to add any further pressure or uncomfortableness for Evan.

When you are sure that he has left, you gather your belongings and head home.

Once at home, you try to relax for the evening, but all you can think about is Evan, and what he may decide to do.

CHAPTER 4

*T*he next day you arrive at work you are shocked to find Evan sitting in your office waiting for you. "Good morning, Evan, it is a surprise to see you here" you respond trying to hide the nervous feelings rising inside of you.

"Good morning, Tori, sorry to ambush you as soon as you arrive, but I needed to talk to you as soon as possible"

"Ok, that is fine, let me close the door," you close the door, take a deep breath, and then sit down across from Evan. "How can I help you, Evan?" you ask, trying to hold back the nerves that are rising inside of you.

"Tori, I am sure you know what I want to discuss with you" Evan responds as his eyes are fixed on you.

"Yes, I am guessing it is about my proposition yesterday," you respond.

"Yes, Tori, it is" Evan responds, his eyes still fixed on you, "I am not going to lie Tori, you proposition was a complete shock, and not at all what I was expecting, I needed time to process your request."

You look at Evan trying to see if you can determine what he is thinking, but his face is not giving anything away. "Evan, I am sorry, I should not have asked you to do that yesterday, it was very unprofessional of me, I apologise for putting so much pressure on you, I…"

Evan cuts you off before you can finish "Tori, I have given your proposition a lot of thought, I have reached a decision, but I want to tell you my decision over dinner tonight, Can I please take you out for dinner at Margie's tonight, say 6.00pm?"

In shock and confusion, you look at Evan, "Oh, Ok, yes of course, you can't tell me now?" you ask.

"I could, but I would rather tell you over dinner" Evan responds.

"Ok, well dinner it is then,"

"Great, I will meet you at Margie's at 6pm" Evan says as he gets up to leave.

"Yes, see you then Evan" you respond, still confused wondering why he could not tell you now.

As Evan leaves, he turns to you, "Have a great day, Tori."

"Thanks, you too Evan."

As you make your way to your desk and start to organise yourself for the day, you ask yourself, "How am I going to concentrate today?" your mind fills with the various scenarios of what Evan may be going to tell you tonight. The sound of your meeting reminder breaks your thoughts, you have an important meeting with a new retail chain today to discuss them stocking your upcoming fashion launch. You are brought back to reality, "Shoot, I have that meeting in about 15 minutes, I better make sure that everything is set for them to arrive". You gather up your important documents and make your way to the meeting room to set up your presentation. As you pass by Evan's office, you notice him hard at work on his latest creation, you think to yourself, "look at him go, he seems really focused."

Several hours later, your meeting has finished, and it has proven successful, the new retail chain will begin to stock your new fashion collection due to be released at the upcoming fashion show in a little over 2 months. This will be a big boost for the company, this chain "Lily's" is a national chain with hundreds of stores across the country, you are excited with the outcome of the meeting but still nervous about the dinner with Evan.

The rest of the afternoon drags on, and you finally leave to prepare for your dinner with Evan, as you arrive home to freshen up, you look at your wardrobe and try to decide what you should wear. Margie's is a pretty stylish restaurant, you eventually decide on your semi formal pink cocktail gown, you fix your hair and make-up and head out to meet with Evan.

As you arrive, the maître d shows you to your table, Evan has already arrived and is dressed in a stylish suit and looks extremely handsome. Evan notices you and gets up, smiles and helps you to your seat. "Hi Tori, you look lovely tonight" he says.

"Thanks Evan, you look great" you say nervously as you take a seat.

Evan pours you a glass of wine, you take a sip.

"How was the meeting with Lily's today?" Evan asks.

"It was really good thanks; they will be stocking our next collection."

"Oh, that is great news, they are such a big retailer, which will be a great addition for the company."

"Yes, it is very exciting" you respond, your mind is focusing on waiting for Evan's decision.

The waiter takes your orders, and you look at Evan, he is looking so calm and relaxed while you are feeling all your nerves on edge waiting for the inevitable discussion.

You both engage in general chatter until the main meals arrive. As you both near the end of your dishes, Evan takes a deep breath and finally begins to broach the subject you have been waiting for, "Tori, let us talk about the proposition you put to me yesterday."

You look at him and reply, "Yes Evan, I am ready, as I said this morning, I am sorry I asked you to do this for me. It was too much; I panicked and honestly did not think it through like I should have …"

Evan interrupts "Tori, wait, let me talk please."

"Sorry Evan, please go ahead" you respond nervously.

"Tori, I will be honest, your request threw me, I certainly wasn't expecting it, I thought all night, I am so honoured that you would think of me to help you with this plan of yours."

You nod your head and brace yourself for the decision.

Evan continues "Tori, I understand how important this company is to you, and during my time with this company, I have seen how hard you have worked to build this company to the wonderfully successful fashion house it is."

You smile at Evan's kind words, "Thank you Evan, that means a lot to hear."

"So, Tori, after much thought, I have reached a decision,"

You feel your heart beating so fast, as you wait for his answer.

"Tori, I will be honoured to help you to keep this company as per your grandmother's requirement, so I will help you to have a baby."

Relief and shock overtake you as you hear Evan's words. "Evan really are you sure?" you ask as tears sting your eyes.

"Yes, I will help you, but…."

The word "but," deflates you, you look at Evan waiting for him to continue.

"Tori, I have to be honest with you, from the moment I started in this company, I have been attracted to you, you are a beautiful woman, so I will help you to have a baby to save this company, but I don't want to go through the sperm donation path,"

The words hit you like a hammer; you look at Evan in shock. "Evan what are you saying?"

"Tori, I want us to conceive this baby naturally, not via the clinical method."

You are not sure how to respond, Evan is an extremely attractive man, but you have not actually thought of him in that way before, all that you can manage to say in response is "Oh, Ok."

Evan continues "Tori, I just want you to know, that I am very grateful for your offer of my own fashion line, I just want you to know that my decision to help you has not been made because of your offer, rather it is because I feel that I have secretly had a crush on you since I started with the company."

You cannot help blush at his confession, "Evan, I had no idea you felt that way."

"Yes, I know, I have tried to hold back my feelings" he says as he reaches for your hand.

"Evan, I am truly flattered, I will be honest, I do find you very attractive, but I am not in the same space as you with my feelings" you say nervously.

"That is fine, Tori, I don't mind, I will be happy to have one special night with you" Evan responds winking at you.

You blush as you continue to eat your meal, a million thoughts running through your mind, you never expected that Evan would confess he had a crush on you, let alone that he wanted to help you fulfill your plan via natural means.

CHAPTER 5

*T*he dinner with Evan draws to a close, you both make your way out of the restaurant and head to the carpark. Before you exit the restaurant, Evan places his arm around you and turns you to face him. He places his hands on either side of your face and passionately encompasses your lips with his. Feelings of warmth fill your body as you sink into his passion and find yourself reciprocating the desire as you wrap your arms around his neck. After what seems likes minutes you both break from the kiss, as you regain your breath, you look at Evan, your legs feel weak and smiling you manage to say "Wow, Evan that was incredible." Evan's face lights up, "Yes, it was," he pulls you in close again and rubs your back firmly sending more passion throughout your body. You find your lips searching for his again and they find their mark and you both share another passionate kiss. Finally, Evan breaks the kiss and whispers to you, "Tori, come with me back to my home and we can continue this."

The passion you are feeling takes control and you answer "Yes, let's go."

Evan leads the way to his car and once inside he pulls out of the carpark and makes his way to his home, you both remain silent as you anticipate what awaits you when you arrive.

As you arrive at his apartment, you crash through the door, engulfed in each other's embrace sharing more passionate kisses, tugging at each other's clothes and before you know it you are both naked and falling on to his bed. You feel a desire that you have never felt before as you caress Evan's taut abs. Evan's hands feverishly caress your breasts, pinching your tight nipples, his hands then move down your body and eventually make their way between your legs where he passionately rubs at your delicate bud, filling you with intense pleasure. Your hands find their way to his length which is hardening with your touch. You guide his hardened length inside you and the intense desire overtakes you and you rock your hips in unison with Evan. Moans of ecstasy fill the room as you both reach the height of excitement.

As you both come back down to reality, you lay in each other's arms catching your breath, there is no need to say anything to each other as you lay caressing each other, eventually sleep envelops you both.

The next morning you wake up, still in Evan's strong embrace, memories of the night before filling your mind and you smile, you have never had such a night of passion and ecstasy. Moments later, Evan awakens and pulls you in close, kissing the back of your head. "Good morning, Tori"

You turn to face him, "Good morning, Evan" and then you reach up to plant a kiss on his lips. Evan responds by kissing you back as he caresses your back. You run your hands over his strong arms and chest, as you do you feel him become hard again, your kisses become more passionate. Evan moves his hand down to between your legs and caresses you, exciting you with every stroke. Evan flips onto his back and lifts you on top of him and you feel his length enter you fully, he thrusts slowly at first, and quickens the pace rapidly, you join him thrusting passionately. Evan gasps as he fills you with his manhood. Smiling you engulf his lips with yours in a deep kiss, rubbing your hands through his hair.

The intense moment is shattered as you hear your phone ring, as you look at it you notice that the call is from Rene, your assistant. You take a deep breath and answer the call "Hi Rene, how are you?" Evan continues to kiss your shoulders and neck.

"Hi Tori, I am just calling to check where you are, you have a designer staff meeting scheduled in thirty minutes."

"Oh no, damn I forgot about that, can you please reschedule, I will be late" you say as you try to think of an excuse on the run, "Sorry Rene, I had an unexpected appointment that I must attend this morning, I probably will not be able to get into the office until mid-morning."

"No problem, Tori, I will reschedule the meeting to tomorrow, is that ok?"

"Yes, thanks Rene, that will be great, please apologise for me."

"Of course, Tori, oh by the way, Evan is not in the office yet, did he mention anything to you yesterday about being late?" Rene asks.

Trying to remain calm you respond, "Oh yes that is right, Evan mentioned to me that he had a medical appointment this morning, he will be in a bit later," you look at Evan and shrug your shoulders. Evan smiles back at you, approving your lie.

"Oh Ok, thanks Tori, funny Evan didn't mention anything to anyone before he left yesterday, Ok, I will let you go to your appointment, I will see you when you get in."

"Yes, thanks Rene, see you later," as you hang up, you turn to Evan and take a deep breath,

"Oh, crap Evan, I can't believe that we have slept in and are late for work."

"Oh well, we were kind of busy last night and again this morning" he responds with a sly smile.

"Evan, we have to get up now and get ready, We cannot arrive at the office together, you need to take me back to my car, so I can drop by home and change before I get to the office" you say as you get out of bed and begin to dress.

"Ok you are right" Evan says reluctantly as he pulls on his pants.

"Evan, I had a lovely night last night, and again this morning, but we need to keep this between us, I am not ready to tell people just yet."

"Oh Ok, sure, if that is what you want" Evan responds as disappointment falls over his face.

"Evan, what happened here was just a means to an end to save my company from my brother Jasper. You are extremely attractive, and I had such a great time, but I am your boss, I don't think it would be appropriate for us to continue other than this baby plan."

"I have a question though, when the plan to have a baby works, what are you going to tell people? Won't our secret come out then?" Evan asks.

You look at him and think, "Honestly, I have not thought that far ahead, I guess I was going to tell people that I used a sperm donor."

"Oh Ok" replies Evan, you can sense his disappointment, he makes his way to the bathroom to have a quick shower and dress for work.

Shortly after, you are back in car, heading back to collect your car that you left at the restaurant the night before.

As you exit Evan's car, you turn to him, "Thank you Evan for agreeing to help me with my plan, and for the wonderful night and morning, thank you" you lean to him to give him a kiss.

Evan responds, "My pleasure Tori, I will cherish last night."

"Ok, see you at work later Evan."

"No worries, Tori, see you later."

As you arrive at the office, you try to sneak in inconspicuously, but Rene spots you, "Oh hi Tori, glad to see you today, how was your appointment?"

"Oh, hi Rene, how are you? My appointment was good thanks, anything happen I need to be aware of?" you ask.

"We received an email from Lily's CEO Grant, confirming the plans for the preorder for the next show, they need your reply by the end of the day."

"Oh ok, I will get on to it soon, everything else, ok?"

"I have rescheduled the designers meeting to tomorrow morning,"

"Oh good, thanks for that, has Evan arrived yet? I need to discuss his design concepts...," just as you ask that, the elevator door opens, and Evan appears. As he approaches you, his face lights up, "Good Morning Tori, how are you? Sorry I am late, I had that medical appointment this morning and as you know doctors always run late, how was your night last night?"

"Morning Evan last night was fine" you reply trying to avoid eye contact.

"Oh, that is good, you must be so excited after the meeting with Lily's yesterday."

"Oh yes, the meeting with Lily's will be great for the company, which reminds me, do you have time to see me in my office to discuss your concepts for the upcoming fashion show?" you ask.

"Of course," says Evan, "Just let me go to my office and grab my folio."

"Great, Ok, thanks" you respond as you turn to head to your office.

A few minutes, Evan enters your office.

"Hi Evan come in and sit down" you gesture for Evan to sit on the couch as you make you way to join him. "Let me see what you have been working on" you ask.

Evan looks at you and asks "Tori, are we going to discuss last night?"

"What do you mean Evan?" you ask knowing full well what he is referring to.

"I had such a great time last night; I can't stop thinking about it" Evan says as he moves closer to you on the couch.

You clear your throat as you look at Evan, "Yes, Evan it was a wonderful night, as mentioned this morning, we need to keep what happened between us quiet for now, I am not ready for everyone to know we were together last night."

"Sure, I understand, but can we see each other again tonight?" Evan asks as he reaches for your hand.

"We will see Evan" trying to change the subject, "We have to start planning the designs for the fashion show, can you show me what you are currently working on."

Trying to hide his disappointment, Evan reaches into his folio and pulls out his designs for you to review. You are extremely impressed with his draft designs "Evan, these are coming along really well, I am loving these."

"Thanks Tori, I just have a few adjustments to make," Evan picks up his designs, smiles and heads back to his office.

The rest of the day goes by quickly and you pack up and get ready for your planned weekly catch up with Lexie. As you enter the local bistro Blue Horizons, you see Lexie sitting by the open fire sipping a cocktail. As you approach, Lexie looks up and smiles, and pulls you in for a hug. "Hey Tori, how are you going?" Lexie asks.

"I am going great Lexie, and you?"

"Yeah, all good, work is pretty busy, exams have just finished for my class, so I will have a lot of marking and report writing to do over the next couple of weeks."

"Oh wow, Lexie, you will be busy then."

"Yes, absolutely, it is a strange feeling that my time with this current class is nearly over, they are a great bunch of kids, I will miss them."

"I understand Lexie, I am sure they will miss you too, just think in a few weeks you will have a new bunch of kids to sort out and bond with."

"That is true, Tori, exciting times, so how are things with you?"

You take a deep breath; a smile appears on your face as you recall the night with Evan.

"I have some interesting news to report" you respond.

"Ooh that sounds intriguing, spill" You take a sip of your mocktail that Lexie ordered for you and begin to fill Lexie in on the events of the last couple of days.

"Firstly, I had a big meeting with the CEO from the fashion chain Lily's."

"Ooh that is big, how did that go?" Lexie asks excitedly.

"Lexie, it was amazing, the CEO, Grant was lovely, and wants to stock our designs."

"That is huge, they are a national chain Tori, congratulations, I am so proud of you."

"Thanks Lexie, it is great news, they will begin stocking our line after our next fashion show in a couple of months."

"That is great news, Tori, you will be busy too then, Oh, how are you going with the baby plan?" Lexie asks giving you a wink.

"Well, I do have an update on that situation" you respond smiling.

"Oh ok, do tell" Lexie says excitedly.

"Well, earlier this week, I went to the sperm clinic and met with one of their representatives, she was very friendly and explained everything it is very expensive, clinical and no guarantee that it will work, anyway, I started the process and set up the profile and received a list of potential donors."

"Ooh, that sounds good, any good ones?"

"Yeah, there were a lot of potentials, but none really stuck out to me."

"Oh, that is no good, what will you do then?"

Well, why I was looking that the donor lists, Evan Thomas walked past my office and an idea came into my head. I wanted to ask him to be my sperm donor."

"What? The fashion designer Evan? he is hot," Lexie asks in shock.

"Yes, he is very attractive, well I explained the situation to him, and I asked him to help me, and he agreed."

"Oh, my goodness, really wow."

"Yes, that is not all, he said he didn't want to go down the clinical sperm donation path, apparently he has had a crush on me, since he started at the firm, and he said he wanted to help me conceive naturally."

Lexie's mouth falls open and she gasps. "What did you say to that?" she asks.

"Well, I said Ok,"

"Wow, I don't know what to say I am in shock, so when will this start then" Lexie asks with a wink.

You blush, "Well truthfully, it started last night actually and again this morning."

Lexie smiles, "Oh really, tell me how it was?"

"Lexie, he was amazing, I had not really thought of him in that way before, but we went out to dinner last night and at the end of the night he kissed me, and wow, is all I can say, we ended up going back to his place and one thing led to another and I ended up staying the night."

"Oh, so what does that mean going forward? Do you have feelings for him now?"

"I do not know Lexie, I am his boss, I don't know what will happen going forward"?

"Oh wow, well it might take more than one night to fulfill your plan Tori" Lexie says giving you a playful slap on the arm.

"Yes, well we will see.'

CHAPTER 6

Several weeks later, you are in your office waiting for Evan to arrive to finalise the designs for the fashion show in a fortnight's time. The last few days you have been feeling a little off, very tired and also feelings of nausea. You have been very busy organising the fashion show and finalising the contract for Lily's, You take deep breaths to settle the nausea, as Evan enters your office with his folio of designs.

"Hi Tori, sorry for the delay, how are you?"

"Hi Evan, I am ok, a little tired, it has been full on finalising this fashion show, how are you going with finishing those designs."

"All good, I have finished the last few adjustments," Evan responds as he pulls out his designs, "Tori, I have adjusted the skirt on this one, to make it fuller, and the neck on this one to make it more streamlined…"

You try to concentrate, but the nausea is becoming more intense, you try to push it aside.

Evan looks at you, "Are you ok Tori? You are looking a bit pale now, can I get you something?"

"I am ok thanks Evan, I will just get my water from my desk" as you stand up, dizziness takes over, and you stumble.

"Tori Be careful, Are you ok?"

"I am ok...." before you can finish, the room starts to spin and you begin to black out, Evan jumps up and catches you in his arms "Tori, I have got you." Just then the room goes dark as you black out completely.

The next thing you remember is waking up in the hospital with Evan by your side.

"Tori, you are awake, how are you feeling?" Evan asks.

"I still feel a bit dizzy, what happened" you ask.

Evan responds, "You collapsed in your office, I rushed you here to the hospital, the doctor is running some tests and will be here soon with the results."

"Oh ok, thanks for staying here with me."

"Of course, I wasn't going to leave until I knew you were going to be ok" says Evan as he squeezes your hand.

"I am sure it is nothing, I have been under pressure lately with the fashion show coming up, I am sure that is all it is" you say trying to convince yourself.

"I am sorry that you were so stressed, is there anything that I can do to help you?" Evan asks.

"Thanks for asking Evan, things are pretty well under control now, just need to get your designs to the sewing department as soon as possible."

"No problem, Tori, I will hand them in to the department tomorrow" Evan smiles.

Just then, the doctor appears in the room, "Hi Tori, how are you feeling now?" she asks as she flicks through the medical notes.

"Hi doctor, I am still a little dizzy and tired. Do you know what is going on?" you ask.

"Well Tori, we have done some tests, and we have the results here" she looks at Evan and then you.

"Oh doctor, it's ok, Evan can stay, I don't mind" you respond.

"Ok, good, well I do have an explanation for how you are feeling, I can confirm that you are pregnant Tori."

Feelings of shock overcome you, "What doctor, are you sure?"

"Yes Tori, there is no mistake" the doctor responds smiling, "Is this expected?"

You turn to Evan, and he is just as surprised as you, a smile appears on his face, you turn to the doctor, "Well, yes and no, I was trying to get pregnant, I just didn't think it would happen so quickly."

The doctor looks at Evan and asks, "This may be presumptuous of me, but are you the father?"

Evan clears his throat and looks at you, you nod, "Yes, Yes Doctor, I am the father."

"Great, so glad I can give you the news together, I will arrange for an ultrasound now to check on things, and then I will get you to stay for a little while longer and then if you are feeling better, I will send you home to rest."

"Thanks doctor, the dizziness is easing a bit now."

"Great, I will get that ultrasound organised, and leave you two alone to process this exciting news."

"Thanks Doctor" you and Evan both say together.

As the doctor leaves, Evan turns to you, "Tori, wow, you are pregnant."

"Yes, Evan, I can't believe it, I really didn't think it would happen so quickly."

The doctor arrives with the ultrasound equipment, the excitement begins to build.

Evan looks at you and whispers "Tori, will it be ok if I stay for the ultrasound?"

You reply, "Of course Evan, this is your baby too," Evan holds your hand tightly as the doctor begins to set up the machine.

"Ok Tori, I am about ready, relax, I will place some gel on your tummy, and we will soon see your little baby. Are you ready?" the doctor asks.

"Yes, Doctor we are ready" you reply.

The doctor places the gel on your stomach, you cannot help jumping slightly at the cold sensation, "Sorry Tori, it is a little cold" says the doctor.

"All good, no problem" you reply.

Just then a small image appears on the screen in front of you. Both you and Evan are fixated on the screen. The doctor says as she points to a small dark object on the screen, "Tori, right there is your baby."

"Oh wow, it is so tiny."

"Yes, I would say looking at this and your blood results you are about 6 weeks along", the doctor replies as she makes some notes on your file.

You feel Evan squeezing your hand tighter as he watches the screen and then asks, "So Doctor does everything look ok with the baby?"

"Yes Evan, everything looks perfect" the doctor replies with a reassuring smile, "Now I will print of an image for you both. Now Tori, I will need you to see an OB/GYN for a check-up every month."

"That will be no problem at all, thanks doctor" you reply.

"Good, how are you feeling now?" the doctor asks.

"Still a little bit tired, but today has been huge."

"Understandable, I would like you to stay for another hour or so before I discharge you home."

The doctor packs up the ultrasound and leaves you and Evan alone with the image of your baby.

"Evan, I can't believe this is happening, thank you so much."

"Tori, it is my pleasure, I am so glad that I could help. I cannot believe that I will soon be a father."

You both spend the next hour or so chatting about the baby and the upcoming fashion show. Shortly after the doctor comes back in, "Hi Tori, Evan, how is everything going now?"

"Hi doctor, I am feeling better now, the dizziness is almost gone now."

"That is great new, well I think I can let you go home now. Do you have anyone at home that can stay with you tonight in case you feel unwell again"?

"Oh, no not really…." before you can finish, Evan interrupts, "I will stay with her, that is not a problem."

"Great, I will write up a referral for an OB/GYN and prepare some information for you and then you will be free to go."

"Thanks doctor" you reply.

After the doctor leaves, you turn to Evan, "You don't have to stay with me tonight, I will be fine."

"Nonsense, I will be there to look after you and our baby, no question."

As you and Evan arrive home, Evan helps you to the couch "Sit here and relax, I will work on getting us some dinner. Can I get you a drink?"

"Thanks Evan, a water will be fine."

"I will be back shortly" Evan makes his way to the kitchen and arrives back with the water. "Here you go, I will whip up some pasta."

Shortly after he comes back into the living room with two bowls of steaming pasta. "Thanks Evan, I was getting a bit hungry to be honest."

As you both eat your meals Evan turns to you, "Tori, now that you are pregnant, I have to say, I want to be a part of this journey with you, I want to be a real father to this baby."

"Evan, I understand how you feel, I am just not sure I am ready for everyone to know you are the father yet."

"Ok why?" Evan asks with a curious look.

"Well, I am your boss Evan, I don't want to cause problems for us in the workplace."

"It is no-one's business Tori; you own the company."

"Yes, I know Evan, I just don't want the gossip and for you to be subject to any ridicule."

"I can handle myself Tori."

"I know you can, I am just not ready for everyone to know yet, but I do want you to be a part of this."

"Just not publicly"

"Not yet Evan, I just need to get my head around being pregnant and fulfilling Grandma's will requirement first."

"Ok, I can work with that, but I am here for whatever you need."

"Thanks Evan."

You both finish your meals and settle in on the couch and watch some television.

"Evan, as I promised in the beginning, for helping me I will arrange for you to have your own fashion line, I will start the process tomorrow ok."

"Thanks Tori, but again, I just want you to know that is not why I agreed to father your child. As I said before, I have had feelings for you for a very long time, I just hope one day you can share the same feelings for me."

You do not say anything, but you squeeze Evan's hand, smile and return to watching the television.

A little while later you begin to yawn and after such a big day you decide it is time to turn in for the night. "Evan, I am going to head to bed now, I will show you to the guest room."

"Thanks Tori"

You both head down the corridor, you reach the guest room door. "This should be comfortable for you there is fresh linen and towels."

"This will be great; I was expecting to sleep on the couch" he looks at you and you become frozen to the spot. Evan moves closer to you and pulls you closer and lifts your chin and kisses you on the lips. You find yourself kissing him back and then suddenly pull away.

Evan senses your feelings "Tori, sorry I got carried away."

"It is ok, Goodnight, I will see you in the morning," you turn and head to your room just a few doors away.

"Goodnight Tori, if you need anything at all please let me know."

"You nod your head, smile and enter your room. As you sit on your bed, you begin to process the events of the day. You cannot believe you are pregnant, that by fulfilling your grandma's wishes the company will be yours. Although nervous about the pregnancy you are also excited, although it is not the way you expected, you have always wanted to be a mother and have someone to care for and fulfill your life. Your thoughts then turn to Evan, you know he wants more from you and although you find him extremely attractive you do not yet have the same feelings for him.

Eventually the thoughts in your head quieten and you fall asleep.

The next morning you wake up, the sun is shining strongly through the window. There is a knock at the door which startles you, you remember that Evan stayed last night.

"Tori, It's Evan, are you awake?"

"Yes Evan, come in" you pull the covers up and try to smooth your hair.

The door opens and Evan enters with a tray of toast, jam and warm milk.

"Good morning, Tori, I have made you breakfast."

"Thanks Evan, how did you sleep?"

"Fine thanks and you?"

"Good thanks" you pick up a piece of toast, but your stomach begins to complain, you cannot hide the feelings from Evan.

"Tori, are you Ok?"

"Yes, my stomach is not great, I will try to eat this and hopefully it will be ok." You manage to keep the toast down and your stomach begins to calm down. "What time is it?" you ask as you look around to your bedside clock.

"It is just after 8.00am"

"Oh no, we have to get to work now."

"Relax Tori, maybe you should stay home today, I am sure Rene can manage things today while you rest."

"Maybe you are right, I am still a little queasy."

"Will you be Ok on your own, do you want me to stay with you?"

"No Evan I will be fine, I will work from home, and start setting up your new line."

"Ok don't push yourself, call me if you need anything ok, I will just clean up the kitchen and head into the office."

"Thanks Evan, I will call Rene now."

CHAPTER 7

Later in the day, you are finishing sending your most recent text message to Evan, he has been checking on you several times today with texts and phone calls.

"Hi Evan, I am finishing the email to the legal team to draw up your new contract for your new fashion line. What do you want to call the new line?"

"I was thinking about calling it Blaze."

"Ooh that is good, I like it."

"Thanks Tori, how are you feeling?"

"I am feeling better now, still a bit tired, but much better than yesterday."

"Oh, that is good to hear, Did you want me to bring over dinner later?"

"No, thanks Evan, I will be fine, I still have a bit of work to catch up on, there is still some of that lovely left-over pasta from last night, I will have that and then I will have an early night I think."

"Ok, don't work too hard, remember I am here for you if you need anything."

"Thanks Evan."

Just then there is a knock at the door, you open the door to find Lexie standing there,

"Oh, my goodness Tori, are you all right? I rang your office today and Rene told me you collapsed yesterday, and you were taking the day off today." Lexie asks as she pulls you in for a hug.

"Hi Lexie, I am fine, come in."

You both make your way to the living room, still anxious, Lexie asks again, "What happened yesterday? Why didn't you call me if you were unwell, I would have come straight away"?

"Well Lexie, I do have news, I was feeling unwell yesterday and fainted while in a design meeting, I was taken to the hospital, and it was confirmed that I am pregnant."

Lexie's mouth drops "What? Oh my god, are you serious?"

"Yes, Lexie it is true, I am about 6 weeks pregnant".

"That is amazing, wait who is the father? Is it Evan?"

"Yes Lexie, Evan is the father"

"Oh wow, I am so happy for you, how do you feel?"

"I am excited, I will fulfill Grandma's wish, most importantly I will have a little baby to look after and fill my life and help fill the hole in my life left by Grandma."

"That is awesome Tori, So does Evan know?"

"Yes, he was with me actually when I collapsed, he took me to the hospital, he stayed with me while the doctor confirmed the pregnancy, then he bought me home and stayed last night."

"What, Evan stayed here with you last night?"

"He stayed in the spare room last night."

"Oh Ok, wow I still can't believe your pregnant with Evan's baby."

"Yes, it is big news, I am still trying to get my head around it all. Evan told me again that he has feelings for me."

"Oh really, how do you feel about him?"

You think for a moment, "Lexie, I am not sure to be honest, he definitely is attractive, I just have never thought about him like that before, plus I am his boss."

"Yes, I can see that would be difficult, but who knows what will happen in the future"?

The next day you are feeling much better and return to work. You decide to call a design meeting, with the upcoming show you feel it would be a perfect time to launch Evan's new line "Blaze."

"Good morning, Tori, how are you feeling today?" asks Rene as you exit the elevator.

"Hi Rene, I am feeling much better today, thank you."

"Oh, that is great to hear, you had us all worried. Any idea what caused you to collapse?"

Not wanting to announce the pregnancy just yet you reply, "The doctor said I had been doing too much and still dealing with the grief of Grandma, I need to rest and take better care of myself."

"Oh, so glad it was not anything to serious, luckily things are going well with the upcoming fashion show so the stress should ease a bit soon. Please let me know if I can do anything to help you."

"Thanks Rene, Can you organise a design team meeting in an hour in the boardroom, also can you please ask Evan to see me in my office now thanks."

"Of course, Tori"

You make your way to your office, saying hello to other staff members on your way. As you reach your office Evan is already there waiting, "Morning Tori, How are you feeling today? Rene said you wanted to see me straight away, is everything ok?" Evan asks worriedly.

"Morning Evan, I am feeling fine, everything is good. I wanted to talk to you before the design meeting this morning about the Blaze line."

"Ok" Evan takes a seat.

"As I mentioned yesterday, I have started the process for creating your new line "Blaze," I want to arrange for the launch to coincide with the upcoming fashion show."

"Oh, wow really, are you sure?"

"Yes, definitely you have the majority of your designs completed, it won't be hard to incorporate them into the new line."

"Tori, this is amazing, thank you."

"So, I want you to work with marketing to design your line label logo etc. I will announce it in the design meeting this morning."

"Ok no problem, Tori, I have ideas already to go" Evan responds excitedly.

"Great, no need to tell you that the next few weeks will be extremely busy. I will need your designs finalised by end of next week to start production."

"Of course, Tori, that won't be a problem at all."

"Great, I will see you in the design meeting at 10.00am".

Evan nods and stands ready to leave, before he does, he turns to you and asks again "Are you sure you are feeling Ok with the pregnancy and all?"

You smile "Yes, Evan things are going well today, I am feeling good today, remember not a word to anyone yet ok."

"Of course, Tori, I am here if you need anything."

"I know, thanks, now I have to get things sorted for the meeting."

"Of course, see you at 10" Evan smiles as he hurries back to his office.

You spend the next 30 minutes sorting out your notes for the meeting.

The time arrives for your meeting, you make your way to the boardroom where all the design team are gathered. You take your spot at the head of the boardroom table.

"Good morning, everyone, thanks for joining me at short notice this morning, but we have important matters to discuss regarding the upcoming fashion show."

Everyone becomes silent and focuses intently as you continue.

"As you know this fashion show is of great significance, our new business partner Lily's will be in attendance and will be heavily focused on our designs as they will be stocking our designs in their stores nationally which is a major step for us."

Everyone smiles, some clap their hands.

"The show is also significant as I intend to launch a new fashion line in this show."

Everyone looks at one another in surprise. You focus on Evan who cannot hide a smile as he looks back at you.

You continue "Yes, I have decided to launch a new line called "Blaze" and this line will be headed by Evan."

All eyes turn to Evan.

"Evan has been with the company for some time now and as our head designer he is the best fit for this new line."

You look around the room and see mixed reactions, most appear positive about the news of Evan introducing his new line Blaze, many congratulating him. As your eyes reach Calvin, you notice his face and can sense anger building up in him.

Calvin has been with the company for just 10 months, a few months less than Evan. "Calvin is everything Ok. Do you have any comments to make on the announcement made today?" you ask.

Calvin seems shocked from his thoughts and clears his throat and replies "No, No I am fine, I am just surprised is all. Evan has only been working here a little longer than me. It is a big step up for him."

"Yes, it is true, Evan has not been here that long, but his designs are impeccable and have proven to be extremely popular with our stockists. He is a strong asset to our business, and I believe now is the time for him to receive some well-deserved recognition" you reply as you look at Evan smiling. Evan meets your eyes and smiles warmly "Thank you Tori for your faith, I promise I won't let you down."

Calvin still visibly annoyed by the announcement, finally extends his hand to Evan "Congratulations mate."

"Thanks Calvin" responds Evan as he shakes his hand.

You all continue to discuss the design deadlines and any concerns that each designer is facing and then end the meeting, so you can all return to your busy schedules.

As you return to your office, Calvin follows you.

"Hi Calvin, is there something I can help you with?" you ask.

"Tori, are you sure that giving Evan his own line is the right thing at this stage?"

You try to hide your annoyance, "Calvin, I appreciate you coming to me, but as I said in the meeting, Evan has more than proven himself with his design capabilities. We could all learn from his talent."

"I understand, but he has only been with the company a little over a year, isn't it a bit soon?"

"Look Calvin, it is my decision, and I believe that Evan deserves this, now is there anything else I can help you with?"

"No, I guess not."

"Great, now let's get back to finalising those designs, shall we?"

"Yes, will do" Calvin responds as he turns to leave. You can sense he is still not happy with the announcement, but you try to put it to the back of your mind as you focus on your ever-growing list of tasks.

Later that day, your phone rings and it is Dean.

"Hi Tori, I am just calling you to discuss the final transfer of your grandmother's house to you. All being well, it should be finalised by the end of the week."

"Oh, thanks Dean, so glad it has all gone smoothly" just then your pregnancy enters your mind. "Oh Dean, by the way I have some news for you."

"Oh yes, what is it, Tori?" asks Dean intrigued.

"It is in relation to Grandma's business transfer requirement, I have just found out that I am now approximately 6 weeks pregnant, so all being well, I will satisfy grandma's requirement."

The phone is silent for a while and then Dean finally responds "Wow, Tori that is huge news, congratulations on the pregnancy, I was not expecting to hear that especially so soon. Can I ask who is the father? I did not know you were dating anyone."

"Thanks Dean, I would rather not say who the father is, it is not relevant, all that matters is that I am pregnant and will satisfy Grandma's requirement."

"Oh, I see, Ok, well the requirement is for a safe delivery of an heir, so there is still a long way to go, but as I said congratulations, I am sure everything will go as planned."

"Thanks Dean, is there anything else you need to finalise the house transfer?"

"No Tori, everything is in order, I will call you at the end of the week once everything is finalised. If you have any questions, please contact me."

"Thanks Dean, all good for now, I will let you go, thanks bye."

"Bye Tori"

You hang up the phone, satisfied in the knowledge that the business will soon be yours. You place your hand on your tummy and murmur softly "Baby, I am so excited for you, you are truly special and will make all my dreams come true."

The next day as you are busily working in your office, your phone rings and the call is from Jasper, before you can even say hello, you hear Jasper's angry voice on the other end of the line "Tori, you are pregnant?"

"Hello to you too Jasper, Yes, I am pregnant, how did you find out? Did Dean tell you?"

"Yes Tori, Dean called me this morning and told me, how can you be pregnant? You do not even have a boyfriend."

"Jasper, it is none of your business how I am pregnant, and how would you know whether

I have a partner or not, we are not close, you wouldn't know anything about me."

"So, tell me who is the father," Jasper voice rises again.

"No, I will not tell you, as I said it is none of your business."

"The hell it isn't Tori, if you have this baby, you will get the company."

"Oh, I see, the real reason for your call, you are worried about losing your stake to this company that you have no ethical right too, you don't do anything for this company, you don't deserve any part of it."

"The hell I don't Tori, it is rightfully half mine, Grandma left it to both us."

"Only if I don't produce a biological heir, which I will now, so the company will be mine as it should be."

Jasper explodes on the other end, "Not if I have anything to do with it, I will fight you Tori, you mark my words" and he hangs up.

His words leave you a bit shaken, what is he going to do, naively you did not expect him to fight the news, you just expected him to accept it. As you are pondering this recent event, Evan appears in the doorway,

"Hi Tori, do you have a moment, I just want your opinion on this skirt design" as he enters your office he looks up and notices the worried look on your face "Tori, is everything ok? Is it the baby?" he whispers.

"No, Evan I am fine, I just got off a rather heated phone call from Jasper, he knows about the baby, and he is less than pleased you might say."

"Oh, well I guess that is understandable to a point, he will lose his free ticket to this company, What did he say?" Evan asks as he takes a seat next to you.

"Evan, he was really angry, and he told me he was going to fight me for the company, I didn't expect that, even by having this baby I could still lose this company," you look at Evan as tears start to form in your eyes.

"Don't even think about that, it won't happen, It was your Grandma's company and she stipulated that you would get this company once you successfully have a baby, it is all going to plan, there is nothing he can do about it, ok."

"I hope you are right Evan; Jasper was so angry."

"Don't worry about him Tori, just focus on this baby" Evan whispers as he puts his arm around you and pulls you in for hug.

"Thanks Evan, I needed that."

Just as you remain in Evan's arms, you hear footsteps and voices outside your office as staff members approach, you quickly pull away from Evan, clear your throat, "Now Evan you had a question about a design" you quickly ask as the staff members walk past, you smile at them in acknowledgement.

"Ah yes, I did Tori, do you think the skirt should be fuller or is this ok?" Evan responds showing you the design.

"It is fine the way it is I think Evan, looks good."

"Thanks Tori I agree I will get it to cutting and sewing department right now" Evan says a little flustered as he stands up and heads out the door.

CHAPTER 8

The day of the fashion show arrives, the last few weeks have been very hectic, you are coming to terms with the pregnancy. You have just passed the 12-week mark, and everything is going well, the morning sickness has settled, and you can notice a very small baby bump appear. You have decided that now the 12-week milestone has been achieved, you will officially announce your pregnancy after the fashion show.

You have not heard anything further from Jasper, so you begin to feel secure that his threats to contest the will were just an empty threat when he discovered the news of the pregnancy.

Evan has been wonderfully supportive and helpful, caring for you as well as successfully preparing for the launch of Blaze, everything is set. As you arrive at the venue, Evan is already there, chatting with the models and putting final adjustments on his designs. As you approach, he looks up, smiles, and walks over to greet you.

"Hi Tori, well the day has finally arrived, I can't believe how well everything has come together."

"Hi Evan, yes everything is looking great for the show, how are you feeling? This is a big day for you, are you ready?"

Evan looks at you, and you can see the excitement in his face as he smiles hugely, "I am so excited, a bit nervous though, I can't really believe that this is happening, Thank you so much Tori, this is incredible."

"You will be fine Evan, you deserve this, I have full confidence in you, you will smash it, you'll see" you reach out and squeeze his arm.

"Thanks Tori, how are you feeling today, how is the morning sickness today?" he whispers.

"I am doing really well today, Evan, the morning sickness is settling down, I am a bit nervous for today to though, but like you so excited."

You leave Evan to perform some final checks on his designs and finalise the instructions for his models and you make your way backstage to check on the other designs. Rene is there and chatting with the rest of the design team and models.

"Hi Team, how are we all going today?" you ask as you approach.

Everyone turns to you smiling, Rene responds, "Hi Tori, we are all great, ready and excited."

"Excellent, that is great to hear, our guests will be arriving soon, all the hard work we have put in over the last few months is about come to fruition, you have all worked so hard, enjoy today" you say in a motivating tone to encourage your team.

"Thanks Tori, we can't wait" everyone claps.

Your eyes meet Calvin's, and you notice him watching you intently. Feeling uneasy, you quickly turn away and head out to the arena where guests are beginning to arrive. You welcome the top fashion reporters and show them to their seats. Just then Grant from Lily's arrive, you make your way towards him, reaching out your hand "Good morning, Grant, welcome to the fashion show, let me show you to your seat."

Shaking your hand, Grant responds "Good morning, Tori, I am excited to be here, please meet my partner Wendy" he gestures to a tall dark head lady next to him.

"Good morning, Wendy, so pleased you could join us."

"Thank you, Tori, Grant has spoken very highly of you and your designs, I can't wait to see them."

"Please follow me" you gesture for them both to follow you to the prime position at the side of the fashion runway.

The time has arrived for the fashion show to begin, all the guests are in place, and the reporters are all prepared with their cameras and notebooks. You make your way to the centre of the stage. "Good morning, everyone, welcome to McIntyre's Fashion show"

The crowd erupt with cheers and claps.

You continue, "We are so glad you all could make it here today, we have all been working so hard over the last few months to produce wonderful fresh designs for you all. I am pleased to announce that during this show, McIntyre Fashions will be launching a brand-new line, called Blaze, which is the creation of our wonderful head designer Evan Thomas, Evan please join me on stage."

Evan makes his way from the rear of the stage and joins you centre stage; the arena is filled with claps and cheers.

"Evan has been with McIntyre Fashions for a little over a year now, and has continually produced wonderful creative designs, so much so that it was time for him to take the next step and have his own line where he can continue to produce the high-quality

innovative designs for which he is well
known. I have no doubt he and his line Blaze
will become a prominent popular player in
the fashion industry."

Evan turns to you and smiles, "Thank you
Tori, and welcome everyone, you are in for a
real treat today. The whole team at McIntyre
Fashions has been working tirelessly to
produce truly impressive designs for you
today and I can't wait to show you my new
line, so please sit back and enjoy what we all
have to offer you."

"Thanks Evan, agreed, sit back everyone,
enjoy the show."

As you and Evan leave the stage, the music
starts, and the first models appear.

As you take your seat at the back of the
crowd, you hear gasps with excitement at
each design as they make their way down the
runway. You hear comments such as "Wow, I
want that," and "That is amazing, that would
look great for my next cocktail party" and "I
love that," each comment brings a smile to

your face, and you cannot wait to tell Evan and the other designers.

The last design finishes on the runway and the crowd erupts with cheers and claps. You join Evan and the rest of the design team on stage.

"Thank you everyone, we hope you all enjoyed our new fashions we have all worked so hard to bring to you today."

The crowd clap and join in a resounding "Yes."

"Thank you all, now we are happy to take any questions you may have regarding our designs, which will all be available for order immediately following the show."

A voice is heard coming from the darkness of the crowd.

"Yes, I have a question, is it true that the only reason the new line Blaze was created is because Evan is the father of your unborn child?"

The words hit you like a hammer, although the voice came from a dark corner of the crowd, there is no mistaking the voice, it is Jasper.

The crowd fall silent, many gasping in shock as they turn to look at each other and then all eyes are firmly fixed on you and Evan. Finally, Jasper appears out of the crowd. "So, Tori, are you going to answer my question, did you promise Evan his own fashion line if he agreed to father your child?"

"Jasper, what are you doing here?" you ask in shock.

"I am here to get answers, I am thinking that everyone here would be interested to know the reason Evan received his own line is because he is the father of your baby, and that the two of you have come up with this plan to steal this company from me."

"Jasper now is not the time to discuss this, I think you should leave now, and we can discuss this later."

"What are you scared that everyone will discover how you tricked Evan into helping you to take what is rightfully mine?"

Evan grasps you hand tightly, and you can sense anger rising in him. Before you can stop him, he stares straight at Jasper. "Look Jasper, I think you need to leave, or we will have security escort you out."

"Oh Evan, I see you are not denying that you are the father of my sister's baby and that you both schemed this up."

Evan responds angrily, "Jasper, as Tori has already said this is not the time to discuss this, Leave now."

"I will not leave until you admit Tori is pregnant with your baby, Evan."

The room is still silent waiting for a response from you or Evan.

After an intense wait, Evan finally answers, "Alright Jasper, Yes, it is true that Tori is pregnant with my baby," you hear gasps from the crowd, "But it is not what you think Jasper, I love your sister, I always have."

"Finally, some truth" mocks Jasper, "While we are on the path of truth, admit that you fathered this baby in return for your own fashion line."

"No, No, Jasper that is not true" Evan responds angrily, "I love your sister, and we are having this baby to stop you getting your grubby hands on this company."

"Evan, Stop please" you say fighting back tears, "Jasper, that is enough, you need to leave now." You turn to face two security guards, "Please can you escort my brother out of here now." The guards nod and head towards Jasper.

Jasper raises his hands in the air, "Alright I am leaving, but this is not over." As the guards reach him, Jasper turns and heads for the exit with the guards following closely behind him.

All eyes return back to you and Evan. You eventually clear your throat and respond, "I am very sorry for that interruption, can we please refocus on the fashion show."

The crowd erupts in a frenzy, multiple hands are raised in the air trying to get your attention.

Trying to compose yourself, you point to fashion reporter Frida who is eagerly trying to get your attention. Frida says "Congratulations on your baby Tori, is it true that your designer Evan is the father? Are you two dating?"

"Hi Frida, thank you, yes Evan is the father, but no we are not officially dating."

"So, what actually is the relationship between you two?" another reporter asks.

"Evan is my head designer" you respond.

"Surely there must be more to it than that?" another asks, "He is the father of your child."

"Evan and my relationship is not something I wish to discuss at the current moment."

"Ok, but surely you can tell us something, like how long have you been seeing each other? When is the baby due? Will you be getting married? What did your brother mean about taking the company from him?"

"All I will tell you is this" you respond trying to remain calm, "Evan is an especially important member of this team and therefore important to me, the baby is due in approximately 6 months so by the end of the year. Our relationship is very new for both of us and not something that we wish to discuss right now. As for my brother's claim, all I will say is that our late grandmother in her will, wanted to ensure succession of her successful fashion company and wished for me to have a child as an heir. Now that is all I would like to say about this topic at this point in time. Can we please return our focus to the wonderful fashion show we have just witnessed. Are there any questions regarding our designs please?" you say firmly.

Reluctantly the crowd refocus on the designs, you can sense that there are still many unanswered questions.

After a pause, Frida asks "Congratulations on a wonderful show, very vibrant and exciting. Where we will be able to find these designs in the retail market?"

"Thanks Frida, yes we are very proud of our new range, they will be available for order immediately from all of our current retailers, plus we are very lucky enough to now have our designs stocked in the national retail chain Lily's", you look at Grant in the crowd, you notice his face, and it appears to be a mixture of excitement but also confusion over what happened with Jasper, You can't help feel concerned and hope that Jasper's outburst has not affected the plan with Grant and Lily's. You make a mental note to ensure that you get to speak to him as soon as the press conference is over.

Another reporter raises their hand, you acknowledge them, "Can I ask what sizes your beautiful designs will come in, will they cater for larger sizes?"

"Great question, all our designs will range in size from 8 – 20, so all sizes will be catered for.

You answer a few more questions about the designs and then decide to wrap up the press conference. "Thank you everyone for joining us here today as we presented our latest designs and launched "Blaze." We trust that you enjoyed the show, and we appreciate your support. Now please help yourself to some refreshments.

The crowd cheer and clap and then make their way out of the arena towards the refreshment tables. You turn to Evan and sigh.

"Oh, I can't believe that Jasper ruined our show like that and caused such as scene." you say to Evan.

Evan responds "Yes, he definitely caused a stir, well the news of the baby is out in public now."

Just then you spot Grant coming towards you.

"Hi Grant, how did you enjoy the show?" you ask.

"Hi Tori, the fashions were as I expected, absolutely fantastic, so fresh and exciting."

"So glad you enjoyed them, we are all very proud of them, we have all worked so hard to produce these new designs."

"Yes, I can see how much effort was put into them.," a concerned look begins to appear on his face. "The outburst from your brother, Jasper, is it? after the show was certainly concerning."

You take a deep breath, "Yes Grant, I sincerely apologise for that, I had no idea he was going to show up."

"Yes well, his claims are certainly cause for concern, as I am sure you can understand Lily's has a very strong reputation to protect, we do not want to be linked to any undue scandals."

Although you are not completely surprised by his comments, you are concerned, "Grant, I certainly understand your concerns, but I want to reassure you that my brother's claims have no merit at all, I apologise again for his behaviour, perhaps we can set up a meeting tomorrow to discuss any concerns you may have, so I can put your mind at ease?"

"I would appreciate that, say 2.00pm tomorrow, can you come to my office? Oh, by the way, congratulations on the pregnancy, extremely exciting news for you."

"Thanks Grant, yes, it is extremely exciting news, I will see you tomorrow at 2pm then" you shake his hand and then return to Evan and the rest of the design team.

CHAPTER 9

The next morning you arrive to the office early, you have scheduled a design team staff meeting to discuss the fashion show and no doubt you expect many questions about Jasper and his claims.

You make your way to the boardroom and find everyone already there waiting, "Good morning glad everyone could make it here today" you say enthusiastically.

"Good morning, Tori" most reply except Calvin.

You take your seat at the head of the table. "Firstly, I want to say a huge thank you and congratulations for a fantastic show yesterday. All your efforts really paid off, the designs were amazing and from the feedback I heard during the show they will be extremely popular. Already when I arrived this morning, we have received multiple orders which is fantastic news."

The group clap their hands at the news.

Calvin clears his throat and speaks over the clapping "Tori, I think we all need an explanation over what happened after the show, with your brother and the claims he has made."

You glare at Calvin, everyone falls silent and stares at you, waiting for you to answer.

You pause for a moment and finally answer "Yes Calvin, of course, Ok, Firstly it is true, I am pregnant."

"Congratulations Tori, that is fantastic news" says Rene and she jumps up from her seat and gives you a big hug, others join in the celebration clapping their hands smiling.

"Thanks Rene, thanks everyone, yes, it is very exciting news."

Calvin interrupts "So it is true that Evan is the father?"

"Yes Calvin, I am the father" says Evan firmly glaring at Calvin.

"Oh, it makes sense now then, your brother was right, Evan was given this new line because you are involved, and you are having his baby" snaps Calvin.

"Calvin as I said before, Evan received his own fashion line because he deserves it, he is extremely talented and ...."

"Yeah Yeah, that is what you said" retorts Calvin.

Evan interrupts "Look Calvin, think what you want, Tori did not give me this line because of the baby. It is true that Tori's late grandmother imposed a requirement on Tori that in order for her to inherit full control of this fantastic company, that she has worked tirelessly in for many years, she needed to have a biological heir to satisfy successful and prosperous succession. I love Tori and we are extremely excited to be having this baby, perhaps earlier than we had planned."

You smile at Evan warmly and whisper "Thank-you."

Calvin rolls his eyes, but remains quiet, but you can sense he is not convinced by Evan's defence.

Rene pipes up excitedly "So are you two officially a couple then?"

You and Evan look at each other, you finally answer "Rene, it is very early days and unexpected, we will see how things progress." You look at Evan and smile, he returns the smile.

"Now can we get back to the fashion show please?" you say to change the subject. "As mentioned earlier, we have had a great response so far, just checking the live report now we have over 1500 units sold to date which is great. I have a meeting with Grant from Lilly's this afternoon, so I am expecting a large order from them this week."

Everyone looks excited.

"Now to finish, unless anyone else has anything to add regarding the fashion show, I want to thank and congratulate everyone again, it is greatly appreciated. However, now is not the time to take the foot of the pedal, we have our next season launch to think about and plan for, so let us get back to work and have a great day."

The room claps and then stand to return to their offices, congratulating you and Evan on the baby as they leave.

"Evan, before you leave can I have a word?" you ask.

"Certainly Tori."

Once everyone has left, you close and lock the boardroom door and you are both alone you look at Evan, "Thank you so much for everything you have done, it means so much to me."

"Of course, Tori, I would do anything for you, you know that" he reaches for your hand and pulls you in close. You find yourself melting into him, feeling his warmth and the rhythm of his beating heart. He kisses you on the top of your head. You move back and your eyes meet. You cannot help but be drawn to him and before you know it, Evans lips crash on to yours and you can feel warmth radiating through your body. You move closer to him wrapping your arms tightly around his back and firmly rub your hands up and down his back feeling his tight taught muscles under his shirt. Evan reaches for your bottom, lifting you off the ground, you wrap a leg around his hips as your kisses become deeper. He places you on the boardroom table, you begin to unbutton his shirt and he lifts your top reaching for your breasts, gently squeezing them. You reach for his belt, unbuckling it and unzipping his pants exposing him. Evan's breaths become faster as he pulls back from the kiss and looks at you, "Tori, are you sure you want to do this here?"

Catching your breath, you whisper "Yes Evan, I want you here right now, the door is locked."

That was all Evan needed to hear, as he pulls your top off and begins to kiss your neck and chest frantically, he whispers, "Oh Tori, I love you so much" as he places his hand between your legs finding your entrance, he gently begins to caress your bud, your body fills with intense pleasure as you open your legs wider, inviting him inside. Without hesitation, Evan enters you and pulls you towards him. You feel a wave of warmth spread from the tips of your toes all the way through out your body as you feel your grip on Evan's back tighten with every thrust. "Oh Evan, don't stop" you whisper before your lips find his again, your tongues intertwine, as your bodies slam together with each thrust. Evan holds his breath as his manhood fills you, he exhales deeply as he rests his head on your chest in an attempt to recover. As you lay back on the boardroom table, you stroke his hair and his back. Finally, Evan lifts his head and looks at you and whispers "Wow, Tori, that was even better than the first time."

You smile back at him, caressing his face "You are amazing Evan."

He reaches up and kisses you one more time.

"Wow, Evan, I guess we better get dressed and get ready for the meeting with Grant."

"Yes, of course Tori, do you want me to come with you?" Evan asks as he helps you to your feet.

"Yes Evan, I would really appreciate that, thank you."

"No problem, I will be there" Evan responds smiling.

As you both redress, you give each other one last approving look, checking your composure before heading to the door.

Later that day you and Evan arrive at Grant's office. The receptionist shows you to the boardroom and you nervously wait for Grant to enter. You cannot help but worry that Jasper's scene yesterday may have caused Grant to change his mind and decide to cancel your business deal. Evan senses your concerns, reaches for your hand, gives it a reassuring squeeze and softly whispers "It will be fine, we've got this" and winks.

Just then the door opens, and Grant and Wendy enter. "Sorry to keep you both waiting, it has been one of those crazy mornings" pants Grant as he stretches out his hand to shake both your and Evan's hands.

"Hi Evan and Tori, great to see you both again" says Wendy smiling as she also shakes both your hands.

"Hi Grant and Wendy, lovely to see you both again, we have only just arrived ourselves" you say as you all take your seats at the table.

Grant clears his throat "Thank you both so much for coming to see us today. Firstly, Wendy and I want to congratulate you both on such as fantastic fashion show yesterday. It was amazing, as I said yesterday, Wendy and I were so impressed with the designs, like nothing we had ever seen before."

"I agree, there were mind blowing" nods Wendy smiling.

"Oh, thank you so much" you reply unable to hide your smile as you look at Evan who is also smiling and you feel some of your concerns ease.

Grant's face then hardens "Now Tori, I have to ask about what happened after the show with your brother Jasper. Can you please explain his claims about the two of you conspiring to take over the company, what was that all about?"

You take a deep breath, "Yes of course Grant, again I apologise for what happened yesterday with Jasper. I will start at the beginning. Our grandmother raised us after our parents were tragically killed in a car accident, after finishing school Jasper decided to pursue an acting career and left us. I decided to support Grandma and work with her in her business. As you know, Grandma suddenly passed away several months ago. In her will she wanted me to inherit the business, but she stipulated that in order to ensure adequate succession, I had to produce a biological heir within 12 months.

Wendy and Grant both raise their eyebrows in surprise.

"Yes, I was taken aback by this requirement also. Anyway, to cut a long story short, Evan agreed to help me hold onto the company and help me to have a baby. Jasper has had no input into this business ever but receives a monthly cut from the profits. I am sure he has no interest in running this business, he just wanted to cause a scene, which he did.

"I see" says Grant "So can I ask was there any truth to the claim that Evan receiving his new line in return for fathering your child?"

"Well…" but before you can finish Evan interrupts "Grant let me answer that please, I will be honest with you, Tori did mention the new line to me when discussing the plans to have a child, but that did not influence my decision to help Tori. As I have said many times, I have loved Tori secretly for so long, so when Tori asked me for my help" Evan turns to you and continues "I thought all my dreams had come true, I wanted nothing more than to be with Tori. I told Tori I did not want the line, but she insisted. I would have helped her with or without the offer of the new line, I just wanted her to see me the way I saw her."

You feel so moved by Evan's words, you feel emotions rise within you, you quickly look away from Evan so as not to allow him to see the tears start to creep into your eyes. You blink the tears away and refocus on the conversation at hand.

"So, Grant, I want to reassure you that there is nothing underhanded going on here. I agreed to help Tori have this baby so she can keep control of this company she has worked in tirelessly for so long. She deserves this company. My decision had absolutely nothing to do with getting my own line" says Evan.

"Ok, well this is a lot of information to take in. I thank you both for being so open with us. I did not mean to pry, I just hope you can understand as I mentioned yesterday, Lily's has a very strong reputation, that we have worked so hard to establish over the last decade, and I will fiercely protect it. I had to make sure that I was not getting involved in any scandals etc that could negatively impact Lily's."

"We understand 100%, I hope you feel more comfortable with what we have discussed today?" you ask.

"Yes, matters certainly are clearer now."

"Good, so does that mean that our business agreement is still on track then?" you ask.

"Look Tori, I understand and appreciate what you have told me here today, but do you think that Jasper has accepted the situation? Do you think he will let things go now or will he pull more stunts like yesterday?"

"Grant, I really wish I could tell you that Jasper's outburst was a one-time thing, but I will be honest with you, Jasper and I are not close at all, Unfortunately, he is a bit of a loose cannon so to speak, I hope that this is the end, but I cannot guarantee that this is over, well not until I safely have this baby and satisfy my Grandma's requirement and legally the company is mine."

"Oh, I see, well that does concern me still, I think Wendy and I need to discuss this between us and weigh up all our options and we will get back to you soon with an answer to our deal."

"Oh, Ok, I understand, is there anything else you need to know to help you make your decision?" you ask trying to hide your disappointment.

"No, I have all the information I need for now, Wendy and I will be in touch very soon. Thank you for coming to see us today, I hate to end this meeting so quickly, but we are on a tight schedule and have to make our way to another meeting very soon." Says Grant as he stands up and shakes your hands.

"Thank you for seeing us today, and we look forward to hearing from you as soon as you make your decision."

You and Evan say your farewells to Grant and Wendy and make your way to the car to head back to the office.

Once inside the car, you look at Evan and unable to hold back the tears any longer, burst into tears.

"Tori, don't cry, it will be alright, Grant and Wendy loved our designs, it will be ok" says Evan as he rubs your shoulder reassuringly.

Through your tears, you say "Evan, I wish I could be as sure as you, I am not so sure that Jasper has not ruined the best deal McIntyre fashions has had, this deal would have put us on the map, made us a household name. I am so angry with Jasper, and dare I say it, I am angry with Grandma for doing this, making this stupid requirement."

"Tori, I understand it is a concern, but Grant and Wendy are not stupid businesspeople, they know how excellent our designs are for them. This deal is just as important to them as it is for us, you wait and see they will not be stupid enough to turn down our designs."

"I hope you are right Evan."

"Of course, I am." Now let us stop and get a hot chocolate before we head back to the office.

"Ok, sounds good, thanks Evan."

CHAPTER 10

*I*t has been a few days since your meeting with Grant and you are trying to remain positive and hoping that Grant will continue with the deal. As you sit at your desk, checking your emails again for a message from Grant, Evan knocks on the door.

"Hey Tori, are you ready to head to the ultrasound appointment?"

"Hi Evan, yes of course, I will just grab my bag."

"Excellent, do you want to grab some lunch after the appointment?"

"Oh yes, that would be lovely" you respond as you join Evan and head to the elevator, you pass Rene on the way, "Rene, Evan and I are just stepping out of the office for a while, we have our next ultrasound appointment today."

Rene smiles "How exciting, take your time, hope everything goes well."

"Thanks Rene, if you hear anything from Grant from Lily's please let him know, I will call him back as soon as we return."

"Certainly, will do, Good luck" says Rene.

Once in the car, you turn to Evan, "I am concerned we haven't heard from Grant yet?"

"Try not to stress to much Tori, I am sure he will call soon," responds Evan.

"I hope you are right, this is such a huge deal, I just hope that Jasper has not ruined this for us."

"As I said the other day, Grant is a smart businessman, he knows how important this deal is for Lily's I reckon there will be an order by the time we get back to the office" responds Evan.

You smile hopefully at Evan.

Evan reaches for your hand "I am so excited to see our baby today. Do you think we will be able to determine the gender today?" Evan asks unable to hide his excitement.

"I hope so, it should be about the time now I think, so Evan, tell me do you have a preference for either a boy or girl?" you ask as you try to think about something other than Grant.

Evan thinks for a moment and then a smile appears on his face "I don't care either way really, but I guess I have always dreamed of having a son to play sports with and go camping and fishing with."

"You do all that with a girl too you know" you reply jokingly.

"Yes, I know of course" Evan responds sheepishly, "So what about you? Boy or Girl?"

"I would be happy with either, but I think I would love to have a little boy too, I can just imagine having a mini you running around."

Evan smiles warmly and as he pulls up at a set of traffic lights he leans across and plants a kiss on your lips.

A little while later you arrive at the clinic and sit waiting for your name to be called. Both feelings of excitement and nerves take over as you will soon be seeing your growing baby on the screen. You move your legs nervously as the minutes seem to tick by. Finally, the nurse appears and calls your name "Tori McIntyre, please come this way" she gestures for you and Evan to follow her into the consulting room. "Good morning the doctor will not be too long, please change here and get yourself comfortable."

"Thanks" you reply as you change, as you climb onto the bed, you reach for Evan's hand, squeezing it tightly "I am so glad you are here with me Evan."

"I wouldn't be anywhere else my love" he replies as he lifts your hand and kisses it gently.

The doctor arrives, "Good morning, Tori and Evan, how are you both doing?"

You reply, "Hi Doctor, I am a bit nervous actually."

"Don't be nervous, just relax and we will have a peek at your little baby" replies the doctor. You lay back and get comfortable, Evan still holds your hand tightly. You both focus on the screen and suddenly the image focuses, and you both see your baby. Evan tightens his grip on your hand as he watches the screen.

The doctor says "Well everything is progressing well; your baby looks perfect. I will take some measurements now."

"Oh, that is great news, Doctor can I ask is it possible to tell the sex yet" asks Evan hopefully.

"Let me see" and after a short pause, "Yes, I can see the gender quite clearly now. Do you want to know now?" asks to the doctor to make sure.

You and Evan look at each smiling, you nod to Evan, and together you both respond to the doctor "Yes please, we would be very excited to know."

"Great, I am pleased to tell you both you are having a very healthy little boy."

Evan squeezes your hand tightly and leans to kiss your forehead.

"Oh, that is wonderful news" Evan responds with a huge smile on his face.

"Yes, that is fantastic" you reply, you feel the emotions begin to take over as tears begin to flow.

"Are you ok Sweetheart?" Evan asks concerned.

You reply still crying "Yes I am fine, just really excited is all."

Evan kisses you on the forehead again and then turns to the doctor and asks, "Is there anything else we need to know at this stage?"

"No everything looks perfect, Tori, how is the morning sickness going?"

"Doctor, things are beginning to settle now, feeling much better now which is a relief, still get pretty tired though" you respond.

"That is normal, just try to relax and avoid too much stress etc" advises the doctor.

"Don't worry Doc, I will make sure she takes things easy" replies Evan looking at you.

"Great to hear, well unless you have any further questions, I will finish then, I will print a photo of your son for you. Congratulations, and keep doing what you are doing, everything looks perfect, and I will see you in about a month unless you need to see me sooner," says the doctor with a smile.

"Thanks Doctor" both you and Evan reply.

A few minutes later, you and Evan are back in the car and heading to the local bistro for a quick lunch before returning to the office. You sit in the car and look at Evan, he is smiling like an excited little boy. Seeing Evan so excited warms your heart, you cannot help but feel closer to Evan and you cannot deny that you are now developing much stronger feelings for Evan.

You reach for Evan's leg and give it a gentle squeeze, he turns to you, you wink at him "How exciting, we are having a little boy."

"Yes, that is great and to know he is growing so well is such a relief."

Just then you arrive at the bistro and spend the next hour or so chatting about and making plans for your son.

As you return to the office and check in with Rene, you and Evan cannot hide your excitement. "We are having a boy!" you blurt out excitedly.

Rene squeals in reply "A boy, that is fantastic" and pulls both you and Evan in for a hug. Almost immediately you are both surrounded by fellow staff members hugging and congratulating you both. You cannot help noticing that Calvin has decided not to leave his desk to acknowledge the news. Although disappointed you are not completely surprised by his response.

As you and Evan finish chatting about the news everyone disperses and you and Evan return to your office, Immediately you check your computer for an email from Grant, you are disappointed to not find anything, just then your phone rings.

"Good afternoon, Tori, it is Grant how are you today?" you hear on the other end of the line.

"Hi Grant, I am very well, glad to hear from you" you usher to Evan to come closer.

"Sorry for taking so long to get back to you, Wendy and I have had a lot to discuss following our meeting earlier this week and we have made our decision regarding our order. We are still a little concerned over the outburst from your brother, however, we are extremely impressed with your fashions so we will be initially placing an order for 2000 units which is half the initial order we discussed during negotiations."

Trying to hide your disappointment, you respond, "I see, well thank you for your order, hopefully it will lead to more orders in the future."

"Yes, well we just want to test the waters first and ensure that the matter with your brother is settled before we invest further, I know it is not what you had planned for, but we just want to remain cautious at this point. I hope you can understand."

"Grant, we are disappointed, but we do understand, I apologise again for what happened with my brother. If there is anything further I can do to reassure you that my brother is not a problem, please let me know."

"Tori let us just see how this first order goes first. Oh, unfortunately, I have to rush off now, I will be placing the initial order by the end of the day."

"Thanks Grant, we look forward to receiving it."

You hang up the phone and turn to Evan, "Oh well, Jasper's plan worked, he has sabotaged the deal with Grant and Lily's."

Evan pulls you in close trying to be reassuring, "Tori, it is disappointing for sure

127

that the order is halved, but on the bright side, there is still an order, so we have to be happy with that. I am sure once they are in their stores, they will fly off the shelves and the next order will be flowing in."

You smile at Evan, "Thank you, you always know what to say to calm me down."

Later in the afternoon Grant's order finally arrives. Evan rushes into your office holding the order in his hand. You can see the excitement in his face, more than 50% of the order is for his fashion line. "Tori have you seen this order? Grant has ordered almost all of my designs."

"Yes Evan, I have seen it, I am so excited for you, you have done a fantastic job and totally deserve this."

Evan pulls you in for a hug and you feel his heart beating fast "Thank you Tori, this means so much to me."

CHAPTER 11.

A month has passed since Grant placed his initial order and you are following Lily's website and social media and are excited to see that sales have been strong, and a significant percentage of Evan's designs have almost sold out online. You feel so relieved and excited for Evan.

As you arrive at the office and begin to set up for the day, you see Evan arrive looking flustered, he rushes into his office, slamming his keys and wallet onto the desk. Concerned you rush over to his office, "Evan are you ok?" you ask.

Evan is pacing about his office and looks at you. "No Tori, I am not Ok, I am really angry."

"Why what has happened?, tell me."

Evan stops pacing momentarily and looks at you, "On the way here this morning, I got a phone call from my building manager, my apartment has been sold and I need to get out by the end of the week." Evan starts to pace again.

"Oh, I see, where will you go?" you ask.

"That is just it Tori, I don't know, and I don't have long to find somewhere else, I have less than five days to get out of my apartment" responds Evan annoyed.

Before you can stop yourself, you blurt out, "Evan come and live with me."

Evan stops pacing and looks at you, "Tori, are you sure?"

"Yes Evan, please come and live with me. Our baby will be here in just over 5 months, so it makes sense that you come and live with me and the baby when he arrives" you reply as you gently stroke your growing baby bump.

Evan stares at you and his face erupts into a huge smile, "Oh Tori, thank you, that would be amazing to live with you and help prepare for our son.," he pulls you in close and kisses the top of your head.

You hug Evan back "Great, then it is settled, you can move in with me straight away."

Again, you see Evan transform into an excited little boy, just like he did when he found out the baby was a boy. "Oh Tori, this is going to be great, I can have my stuff packed up in no time, and we can work together on setting up the nursery together, and I will cook dinner for you every night, and look after you……" You cannot help but smile as you watch him and listen to him as he begins planning the move and preparing for the baby.

At the end of the day, you follow Evan back to his apartment and start helping him pack up. As you pack the last of his boxes in the cars, you feel relieved, "Well, that didn't take so long, we can organise a removalist to come and get the big stuff tomorrow and then we are all set."

"Thanks for your help, Tori, I couldn't have done it without you."

"My pleasure Evan let's get going home."

"Home, I like the sound of that" Evan says as he wraps you in his arms and melts you with one of his kisses.

Shortly after you arrive home and begin to unpack the cars. Evan begins to carry his boxes into the spare room. "Evan where are you going with those?" you ask.

"I am heading to the spare guest room" he responds confused.

"No, put them in my room, I mean "Our" room."

"Are you sure?" Evan asks.

"Yes, Evan, I want you to share my room with me," as you lead the way to the master bedroom and begin to clear space in the wardrobe for Evan's belongings.

Evan follows you excitedly, "Oh Tori, I can't believe that you want me to share the room with you, are you really sure you are ok to take this next step?"

You reach for Evan's hands and squeeze them tightly as you look into his eyes. "Yes Evan,

132

I am sure, the last few months, I have been drawn closer to you, you are amazing, and I honestly feel that I am falling in love with you."

Evan picks you up in his arms and twirls you around, a smile beaming from his face so brightly, "Oh Tori, I love you so much, I never thought that you would ever feel as strongly for me as I do for you", Evan responds before crashing his lips onto yours with a passion that fills you warmly from your toes all the way through your body.

The next morning as you lay in bed encapsulated in Evan's strong arms, feeling the rhythm and warmth of his breathing and the warmth of his body behind you, you begin to smile contently, enjoying the security of having Evan in your life and the impending arrival of your new baby boy in a few months. Your life is perfect now.

Your thoughts are broken by the sound of the doorbell and strong knocking on the front door. You and Evan both jump up startled and throw on clothes as you rush to the door. You open the door to find a legal courier standing in front of you. "Good Morning, Tori McIntyre and Evan Thomas, you have been served, Have a good day" he says as he thrusts envelopes to both you and Evan and turns and leaves.

You call out to him "Wait, what is this?" but he continues to his car and drives away.

You and Evan turn to each other "What the hell is this? And how the hell did he know I would be here this morning?" Evan asks as he closes the door and focuses on the envelope in his hand.

"I have no idea Evan" you respond nervously as you proceed to the living room and open the envelope.

As you pull the paperwork out you read the top and see it is Notice of Intent to Contest the Will of Esther June McIntyre. "What the hell, Jasper is going to contest the will?" you exclaim in shock.

"Bloody hell, what is he up to, and what has that got to do with me" Evan asks as he opens his envelope to find a Notice of Intent to Raise an Injunction on Blaze Designs "No, what the hell, how can he do this?"

"Evan, I am sorry, I never thought he would do this, I really thought as we hadn't heard from him since the show, it was over."

Just then your phone rings, "Hey Sis, I see that you have received my surprise delivery" Jasper laughs wickedly.

"Jasper, what the hell are you up to?" you respond angrily.

"You thought that you and your little boyfriend were going to win in cutting me out of what belongs to me, well I am not going to let that happen" retorts Jasper.

"You are not going to win Jasper, I will fight you on this, this is not what Grandma wanted, you have not shown any interest in this company ever, you have no right to any of this."

"We will see about that, so I see that your little boyfriend has moved in with you now."

"Wait how did you know about that?"

"Oh, I know a lot sister, don't you worry about that, enjoy it while you can, I am going to win, and the company will be mine" claims Jasper and then hangs up before you can respond.

Evan paces around the living room, "Why is he doing this, we have to stop him Tori, it will ruin Blaze Designs and McIntyre Fashions."

"I know, I will call Dean immediately and get this sorted out."

You and Evan arrive at Dean's office to discuss the legal papers Jasper has sent. "Dean, Can Jasper do this? we have to stop him."

"Let me have a look at these papers" Dean asks as he reaches for them and starts to read them.

He finally finishes and looks at you with a concerned expression "I am afraid these papers are legal, as you have not yet safely delivered your baby to satisfy the will requirements, Jasper is well within his rights to contest the will."

"Bloody hell Dean, what can we do about it and what about Blaze Designs?"

"Yes, well unfortunately, as the full ownership rights to McIntyre Fashions is still not fully resolved, major changes such as launching new design labels must be approved by both parties, that is you and Jasper."

"Dean we have to fight him on this, it will ruin McIntyre Fashions." You say to Dean concerned.

"I understand Tori, leave it with me, I will carry out some investigations" Dean responds.

"So, what do we do about the injunction Dean, we have close to a million dollars of pending orders right now." Evan asks.

"Yes, that is a concern" Dean looks at the injunction notice and then smiles "Ok, there is a loophole I can see that we can exploit."

You and Evan look at each other and focus intently on Dean "Go on what is it?"

"I see that the injunction is not immediate rather it is to take effect from the 20th of the month, which is 1 week away. So, you still have 1 week before the injunction takes effect. This is extremely poor legal advice by Jasper's legal team, so as I see it you still have 1 week for Blaze designs to trade."

"Oh, that is good news, we can get a lot of those order out within that time frame for sure" you say smiling as you think of how to make this work.

"Good, make the most of this week then, as I said, this is a major fault on behalf of Jasper's legal team to leave this loophole, very bad business for their client," Dean responds shaking his head, "But great news for you!"

"Thanks Dean, please do what you can to stop the injunction from taking effect next week and avoiding Jasper contesting the will please."

"Of course, Tori, I will be right on to it now and be in touch as soon as I can."

You both shake Dean's hand and leave to head back to the office.

As you arrive in the office, you ask Rene to organise an urgent design team meeting with all the sewing and design teams.

Once everyone has arrived for the meeting you begin to explain the legal situation with the impending injunction.

"Hi team, thanks for joining me at such short notice, I believe in being transparent, we have been made aware of some potential legal issues surrounding Blaze Designs. This will affect our ability to fulfill our orders past next week. Therefore, I am requesting a huge effort from each and every one of your to fulfill the current orders as soon as possible before this legal complication takes place. So, team, what I am requiring is for the next week we will all be required to work overtime to get these orders out ASAP."

You look around the room at your team and notice mixed reactions, "Team, I know this is a big ask, but I really need your support on this. As mentioned, it will be paid overtime. Does anyone have any questions or concerns?"

Calvin raises his hand "So what has caused this situation?"

"Calvin, in wanting to stay transparent, I will tell you all that unfortunately my brother is causing some legal problems for us, but our legal team is on it as we speak so I am sure it will be resolved quickly.

Your head sewer Helen asks, "How much overtime are we talking?"

"I need everyone to put in as much time as they can, I understand that you all have families, but I cannot stress to you how important it is to get these current orders out as soon as possible."

Helen responds, "Do not worry Tori, we have your back, we will do what is needed to get the job done."

"Thanks everyone, I really appreciate your support, you are what makes this company what it is, unless anyone else has anything to raise, I will end this meeting and we can all get stuck into smashing these orders out."

Everyone heads back to their workstations.

The next week is spent supervising everyone to ensure that the orders are met, as well as assisting with sewing, packaging and invoicing. As the deadline for the injunction approaches you are pleased to discover that you and your team have been able to fill almost 95% of the order list.

Evan joins you in your office. "Evan, we did it, we achieved 95% or our orders before the injunction starts" you say as you flop on the couch.

Evan joins you "It is amazing we achieved so much, we have a great team."

"That we do for sure. I wonder how Dean is going with the legal stuff with Jasper. I have been so busy this past week, I have not had a chance to follow him up."

Just then your phone rings and it is Dean.

"Hi Tori, it is Dean here, I just wanted to give you an update on the legal matters with Jasper."

"Hi Dean, how are things going?"

"Well, I wish I had better news for you both. I have been unable to prevent the injunction from coming into effect today. Jasper is claiming impropriety on the grounds that Blaze Designs was created as a result of the relationship between you and Evan and your impending baby."

"Oh no Dean, that is so unfair" you respond.

"I know Tori, but unfortunately the timing of your pregnancy and the release of Blaze Designs is too much of a coincidence."

"So, is there anything we can do Dean?" Evan asks.

"Evan, unfortunately not at this stage, unless we can prove impropriety on Jasper's side then we are stuck, until the contesting of the will is sorted." Dean responds.

142

Evan rolls his eyes in disbelief and begins to pace the office.

You think for a moment, "Dean you may have a point I had not considered." Evan stops pacing to look at you.

"What are you thinking?" asks Dean.

"Well, for years Jasper wanted nothing to do with this business and now all of a sudden, he is showing an interest, and wants half. He is already getting a portion of the profits regularly; it seems odd to me that he is claiming he has rights now. He is up to something; I just wish I could work out what it is."

Dean responds, "You do have a point I guess, for years he seemed satisfied with the generous monthly distributions, Now he seems to want more. Do you really think he has sinister motives for wanting this business?"

"Look, with Jasper anything is possible, he may be my brother, but I really have no idea what is going on in his life. When it came to

Grandma and me, he was a closed book, never letting us in on his life at all."

"Ok, well let us see if we can find anything that may explain the sudden interest Jasper has, I will carry out some investigations and see if I can uncover anything" says Dean.

"Thanks Dean, we will do the same" you respond as you hang up the phone and look at Evan.

"Well Evan, we need to see if we can determine why Jasper wants this company so badly" you say but are unable to hide a yawn.

"True, Darling, but right now, I want to get you home, you have worked like a trojan this past week and you and the baby need to rest" says Evan stretching out his arms to help you up from the couch.

"Yes, you are right Darling, I am pretty tired now, I would love to go home, have a bubble bath, get in some takeaway and crash on the couch with you watching some trashy TV."

"Sounds great to me, let's go home" Evan says as he pulls you in for a hug "I love you Tori, so much."

"I love you too Evan" you respond catching Evan off guard. He was not expecting you to confess your love to him. Smiling he crashes his lips onto yours and squeezes you tightly.

You make your way home and have a wonderful peaceful night-in enjoying each other's company.

CHAPTER 12

*T*he next morning you wake to sunshine filling your room and the sounds of birds happily chirping outside the window. As you lay in bed cuddled into Evan's strong arms mixed feelings fill your mind. You are happier than you have been for many years, content in the knowledge that you have found a wonderful man to share your life and home with and that in just a few months you will be welcoming your new little boy into the world and beginning a new chapter of your life as a mum. These thoughts are then tinged with the realisation that Jasper is standing in your way of achieving this amazing life that you have dreamed of ever since you can remember. Instead, Jasper wants to destroy everything you have worked so hard for and destroy not only your dreams but the hard work and dreams of Evan. You cannot help but feel guilty, Evan has worked so hard to create Blaze Designs and now because of your brother, all his hard work and his dreams are threatened also. Tears begin to tear at your eyes, you quickly brush them away and try to get out of bed to wash your face. As you sit on the edge of the bed, tears still staining your face, Evan stirs, "Good Morning, Darling, where are you going?" he asks wearily.

You do not want him to see your tears, so you do not face him, instead you say "Oh good morning, sorry I woke you, I am just going to go to the bathroom" your voice is unable to hide your emotions fully and quivers slightly.

Evan sits up and puts his arms around you from behind, "Darling, are you ok? Is something wrong?" he asks concerned as he kisses and strokes your hair.

You try to remain strong, but the tears continue to flow, "I am ok, just all this crap with Jasper is getting to me I guess."

Still holding you tightly, Evan whispers "It will be alright, we will find out what he is up to and stop him."

You turn to Evan, and he sees your tears and begins to wipe them away. "Evan I am so sorry, for everything, if it was not for me and my baby idea, you would not be in the situation where you can lose Blaze Designs and everything you have worked so hard for" you cry.

"Hush" says Evan, "You have nothing to apologise for darling, I knew what I was doing when I agreed to help you, you have made me the happiest man on earth, I cannot believe my luck that I am here with you and our beautiful baby boy that is growing inside of you. I have everything I could want darling."

"But what about your design label? Jasper is taking that away from you, you do not deserve this, you are so talented, and this is all my fault."

Evan kisses you and replies "Sure what Jasper is doing sucks, but I do not care, it means nothing to me without you and our son, that is what I want more than anything."

"Oh Evan, you are so sweet to say that, but it has always been your dream to have your own label."

"It was until I met you, you and our baby are my dream now darling" Evan responds and then kisses you deeply.

You and Evan spend the rest of the day, discussing how you can investigate Jasper and his sudden interest in McIntyre Fashions. "We need to think like the police Tori, how would they investigate someone?"

"Your right Evan let's think about this" you ponder.

After a while of deep thought, Evan asks "What do you know about Jasper? Do you know any of his friends, his interests, anything"?

"Unfortunately, not, Jasper never confided in Grandma and I very much if at all" you respond with a sigh. "

"Ok do you know if Jasper is on any social media. Maybe we could see if he is posting anything about his interests etc."

"I will see if I can find something, let me have a look" you take out your phone and try to find Jasper on Facebook etc. "Ooh there he is, let me see if he has posted anything useful" you say as you scroll through Jasper's page. "Oh, he is quite the social butterfly isn't he, lots of photos of him drinking with groups of people. Wait what is this, that person right there in the background looks a lot like Rene," you say in astonishment as you pass the phone to Evan.

Evan studies the photo, "It is hard to tell really, it looks a bit like her, but the photo is a bit dark and there are a lot of other people in the way, Rene does not know Jasper, does she?" Evan asks.

"I don't think so, she has never mentioned him before" looking at the photo again, you say, "you are right the photo is not great, I am sure it is not her."

You keep scrolling, "Well there is not much here, just lots of parties, and drinking. Ooh, these people look a bit rough" you show Evan a photo of a group of men covered with tattoos on motorbikes with alcohol.

"Ooh yeah, they look a bit rough don't they." says Evan raising his eyebrows.

You turn to Evan "I still think Jasper is up to something. The timing of all this is just too much of a coincidence."

"Yes, as you say, he has never shown any interest in the business before. He seemed to be happy enough to sit back and receive his regular profit distributions for no input at all" Evan responds.

"That is right, I do not understand what has changed and why he is so interested in getting involved in the operations of this company now."

Evan ponders for a moment, "Do you think he has gotten himself involved in something shady?."

"Oh, I do not know, I certainly hope not" you respond worriedly.

"Do you think we should hire a private investigator of sorts to follow him and see if they can find something out of the ordinary?" Evan suggests.

You think for a moment and then respond "Truthfully, I was thinking the same thing, I hate having to do this to my own brother, but we need to find out if he is up to something before it is too late."

"Ok then, well let's organise this as soon as possible."

The next day you and Evan meet with Mario from "Discrete Observations. You welcome Mario into your home and open the conversation, "Hello Mario, thanks for coming to meet with Evan and myself, we are hoping that you can assist us with the matter regarding my brother Jasper we discussed on the phone yesterday."

"Hello Tori and Evan, I am very pleased to meet you, now as discussed you are concerned about your brother's intentions regarding your business McIntyre Fashions."

You nod in reply.

Mario continues "Ok now I will need to ask a series of questions to get a better understanding of the situation and Jasper in particular. Tell me what you can about Jasper."

"Ok, well Jasper is my older brother, unfortunately we are not close, our parents died many years ago when we were both kids. Our grandmother raised us both and when he turned twenty-one, he moved away to follow an acting career."

Mario takes down notes and stops to ask, "You say that you are not close, can you clarify how often would you say you connect or keep in touch?."

"Mario, I have to confess, since he moved away, I don't have any contact with him, he rarely visited Grandma and I. I would say since leaving about 8 years ago now, he has probably been back a handful of times. On those occasions it would only be a very brief catchup, a dinner etc and he would not discuss anything personal with us."

"Ok, so you mentioned he left to pursue an acting career, would you say he is successful? Has he been contracted for much?" Mario asks.

"He has had a few small roles, but mostly commercials, no leads in movies or TV as such."

"Ok, so I am guessing that you would not know much about his personal life, friends partners etc.?"

"No unfortunately not, he does not share that kind of information with us. I only know what I see on his social media accounts."

"Ok, I will look into that and see if anything flags of interest. I will also conduct some undercover monitoring of his movements and check into his phone records also."

"Thanks Mario, I have to ask, I do not mean to pressure but how long do you think it may be before you are able to find anything? As it is affecting our business operations, time is critical. Also, we would appreciate the matter resolved before our baby arrives in a few months" you say as you caress your growing baby bump.

"I understand perfectly Tori, I will start right away, and this case will have my full undivided attention, so I will do my best to get answers for your as soon as possible" Mario responds smiling as he stands up to leave. "I have lots of information from today's meeting and what you provided me yesterday. I will be in touch as soon as I can."

"Thanks Mario" you shake his hand and escort him out. As you shut the door you and Evan look at each other and raise your eyebrows "Oh well that is it now, hopefully he will find something to help us" you say as you reach out to Evan. Evan pulls you in close, kissing the top of your head. "Mario is the best in his field, if there is something to find, he will find it for sure" Evan whispers to you as he tightens his embrace on you.

You and Evan spend the rest of the day together planning the nursery for your new son and trying to take your minds off the Jasper situation.

The next day as you and Evan arrive at the office and are parking the car, you and Evan notice Rene pacing the car park while on her phone in what appears to be a very heated conversation. As you get within earshot you hear Rene say "Alright, I will do what I can, don't pressure me ok." Just then she looks and notices you and Evan, she quickly ends the call. "Oh, good morning you two, how are you both?" she asks smiling as she tries to compose herself after the phone call.

"Good morning, Rene, is everything Ok?" you ask.

"Yes of course, why do you ask?" Rene replies quizzingly.

"I did not mean to overhear, but you seemed to be in a pretty heated phone conversation just now."

"Oh that, that was just my sister, we are planning an anniversary party for our parents, and she is pressuring me with plans" Rene responds with raised eyebrows.

"Ok as long as everything is ok" you say as you place a reassuring hand on her arm.

"Yes, yes everything is fine, thanks Tori" Rene says as you all head inside and prepare for another busy day.

Although the injunction is now in place, Evan continues to mentor other designers and work on designs to be included under the traditional McIntyre design label. You walk by his office and watch him deep in concentration on his next creation. As you stop and watch him work, he seems to sense your presence and looks up to meet your gaze, smiling he says, "Oh hey sweetheart, what can I do for you?"

Smiling you respond "Hi, you look busy, can I see what you are working on?."

"Oh, not yet it is not ready yet, I am not ready to show anyone yet" he responds as he turns the page on his design book.

"Oh Ok, no problem" you are a bit surprised as Evan has not withheld his designs from you before, you cannot help but be intrigued to know why he will not show you this design yet, but you decide to respect his wishes.

A week later, your phone rings and Mario is on the other end of the line "Hey Tori, I have some important information I need to share with you, can we meet up this afternoon?"

"Hey Mario, that is great news, yes of course, do you want to meet at my office after lunch?" you ask.

"It would be better if we can meet elsewhere, can you meet me at the coffee shop 'Little Beans' in 2 hours.

"Ok sure, Evan and I will be there, thanks." You hang up and head to Evan's office to tell him the news.

As planned, you and Evan head to meet Mario, as you enter the coffee shop your mind is running overtime wondering what Mario has uncovered. You anxiously watch the door, finally Mario enters and make his way towards you.

As he reaches your table he smiles and shakes both yours and Evan's hands "Hi Tori and Evan, thanks for meeting me here today. I have found some interesting information I want to share with you."

You feel your nerves rise as you listen to Mario intently.

Mario continues "I have been able to track Jasper's movements and investigate his phone calls for the past week. Interestingly I discovered a recurring number showing in his phone logs almost daily, sometimes multiple times a day. Do you happen to recognise this number?" Mario asks as he shows you both details of a mobile number. You and Evan study the number closely and then you gasp in shock "Oh my god, I know that number, it is Rene's number!" you exclaim in shock.

Evan asks angrily "Why would Rene be communicating with Jasper?."

"I do not know Evan; I am just as confused and angry as you are" you respond.

Mario asks "Rene is your assistant? Is that right?"

"Yes, she is, she has been with us for the last 5 years. I know this is a big ask but were you able to determine what Rene and Jasper were discussing during these phone calls and texts?" you ask.

Mario's face hardens "Yes, we were able to track the text messages, I am sorry guys it appears that Jasper and Rene are having a romantic relationship, there was some quite explicit texts which I will not share."

"What! I did not even know that Rene knew Jasper" you say with exasperation.

"Yes, our records show that this has been going on for at least the last 5 months".

"About the same time your grandma passed away and she made the requirement in her will" Evan says.

"Oh no, is Jasper using Rene to get to me and this company?" you ask.

"I am not sure of his motives at this stage Tori, but I will say that from the texts, Rene is definitely feeding him information about you both and the company" explains Mario.

Anger rises in you "Rene is spying on us for Jasper, Oh my god, how could she do this to us."

"The little witch, wait till I see you her tomorrow" Evan says fuming.

"Evan, I know how angry you are, but I advise you strongly to remain calm. You cannot under any circumstances let Jasper and Rene know what we have uncovered" urges Mario.

"What, we can't let her get away with this" Evan says.

"We won't Evan, we need to keep this connection between Rene and Jasper going, to gather more information for our case."

Reluctantly you and Evan look at each other and nod in agreement. "Alright, we will remain silent, but it will not be easy" Evan responds sternly.

You clear your throat and ask "Mario, did you find out anything else about Jasper and why he might be doing this to us?"

"Well yes Tori, I have found out something else, it is not good news unfortunately Mario says.

"Really what is it?" you ask, concern fills you.

"Tori, I have been following Jasper for the last few days and I hate to inform you, it would appear that he has gotten himself involved with a pretty dangerous crowd."

"What do you mean dangerous?" you ask.

Mario continues "I have seen him meet up several times with a group called the 'The Hopper Royals,' they are a pretty nasty group, involved in drugs, organised violent crimes you name it."

"Oh my god, how did he get involved with them?" you ask.

162

"Tori, I am not exactly sure of the extent of his connection at this stage, but I do know he has made and received multiple calls and texts from gang members. On one of my surveillance operations, he was followed by some of the members and appeared to have a heated interaction. I am still having Jasper followed and need a little more time to come up with something more concrete" explains Mario.

"You have done an amazing job so far Mario, in such a short time. The information on Rene and now the gang interaction is proof he is up to something for sure" says Evan.

"Yes Mario, Evan is right, you have done an amazing job, thank you" you say smiling.

"Thanks guys, I still have a lot of work to do, so I will end this now and get back to it."

"Of course, thanks Mario" you both shake hands with Mario and watch him leave.

Evan turns to you and asks, "How are you feeling after what Mario has just told us sweetheart? Are you ok?."

"Evan, I am in shock to be honest, it is so much information to take in" you reply taking in a deep breath.

"I know sweetheart, I cannot believe that Rene is betraying us like she is, I am so angry" says Evan, you can sense the anger in his tone.

"I know, we trusted her, oh my, the information she knows about the company and us. I shudder knowing that she has been running to Jasper with all our private details" you say shaking your head.

"Well, what are we going to do about her, I know what I want to do" says Evan.

"I am angry too believe me, darling, but we have to follow the guidance of Mario and as hard as it will be, we cannot let her know we are on to her."

"Yes true, Ok, it will be hard though."

"Do not worry, her time will come when this is all over believe me" you warn.

"What will you do, will you fire her?" Evan asks.

"Yes definitely, she has lost my trust now for sure" you reply.

"Ok good, now we know what she is up to, we have to be careful and not give her much ammunition to take to Jasper" says Evan.

"Yes true, but it will be fine line, we cannot give her access to important information, but we cannot cut her off completely as she may get suspicious."

"We will work it out" reassures Evan, "How do you feel about the gang involvement?"

"Oh Evan, that is awful, how could he have gotten involved with such a dreadful crowd. Even though he is doing this to us, he is my brother, I love him, and I am scared for him."

Evan puts his arm around you and your tears begin to flow, "I understand sweetheart, it certainly is a worry, hopefully Mario can get the information he needs and maybe it can

help Jasper get himself back on track." Evan
strokes your hair as you cry into his shoulder.

CHAPTER 13

A few days have passed since your meeting with Mario, you are heading home after meeting up with Lexie. She was stunned to hear the updates on Rene and Jasper. As you turn into your street you begin to feel relaxed for the first time since meeting with Mario. Lexie has always been a big support to you and being able to let everything out to her during your catch up has really helped.

As you open the door and enter your home you are met with the most amazing aroma, your favourite meal, roast beef, is cooking. You find Evan in the kitchen hard at work, checking the roast beef and vegetables in the oven. As he closes the oven door he turns around and jumps as he is startled to see you standing there. "Hey sweetheart, you are home, I did not hear you come in" he says as he catches his breath from being startled.

You head over to him crash your lips on to his "Hey darling, sorry to startle you, what is all this then?" you ask as your eyes scan the kitchen all Evan's hard work and then you notice the dining table perfectly set with candles, flowers and your grandma's special crockery.

"I wanted to make you a special dinner tonight, you deserve it sweetheart" he says smiling.

"Oh, darling that is so sweet, what can I do to help?" you ask as you roll your sleeves up waiting for instructions.

"No, No you just relax, I have got this, dinner will be ready soon, just go and change into the special outfit I have set out for you."

"Really, you have an outfit set out for me, how exciting, you are spoiling me tonight aren't you?" you say excitedly.

"Always my darling, get used to it, I will spoil you each and every day I promise you that" Evan says as he kisses you and then turns to point you towards the bedroom "Now go and get ready" he says as he gently pats you on the behind smiling.

"Ok I am going" you say as you eagerly make your way to the bedroom. As you enter the doorway you are met with the most amazing sight. Evan has laid out the most amazingly special red and gold sequinned dress. As you put on the dress, it fits perfectly, and you feel like a princess in the long flowing gown.

As you make your way back to the kitchen you find Evan now dressed in a suit and dinner waiting for you. Evan smiles as he sees you enter the room. "Sweetheart your look absolutely beautiful, come and sit down, dinner is ready now" says Evan as he pulls out the chair for you.

"Wow Evan this is incredible, what are you up to?" you ask trying to work out what is going on.

Not giving anything away, Evan responds as he sits down across from you. "I just want us to have a special dinner tonight."

He asks you about your catchup with Lexie, you tell him how relieved you felt after sharing recent events with Lexie and how she helped you feel more relaxed now.

"Oh, that is great to hear sweetheart, so glad you had a good catch up" Evan says.

As you finish you main course Evan clears the dishes. When he returns to the table you sense his mood has shifted slightly, he appears to be a little anxious, you notice him fiddling with the tablecloth and his glass. "Sweetheart are you Ok? You look a little tense or anxious, is something wrong?" you ask.

Evan looks at you with a nervous smile "I am ok, but there is something I want to ask you though."

"Ok for sure, you can ask me anything" you respond.

Evan takes a deep breath; he gets up from his chair and moves around the table towards you. Once he reaches you, he reaches for your hands and gently turns you to face him, still holding your hands he then kneels down on one knee.

You begin to sense what may be happening and your heart starts pounding strongly, almost out of your chest.

Evan takes another deep breath, his eyes meet your, his voice suddenly starts to quiver slightly "Tori, the last few months have been the happiest of my life. You are everything I have dreamed of, you are funny, absolutely amazingly strong and the most caring and loving woman I have ever met, not to mention the most beautiful and sexiest woman ever. I cannot believe that in a short five months we will be welcoming our son. You and our son are absolutely everything to me. Tori McIntyre will you make me the happiest man in the world and do me the honour of becoming my wife?"

Emotions being to fill your body, you are in shock, you were not expecting this to happen tonight. Happy tears begin to sting your eyes, your heart is pounding even harder. You cannot hold back the tears any longer, you smile widely, and you squeeze Evan's hands tightly "Oh my god Evan, Yes, Yes, I will definitely marry you" you say almost squealing with excitement.

Evan suddenly smiles as your answer registers with him "Yes Tori, you said Yes?" he asks.

"Yes Evan, I will be your wife, definitely."

Evan gets to his feet, lifts you from your chair, pulls you in tight, lifts you up off the ground and swings you around in an excited twirl. As he plants your feet back on the ground, his lips crash on to yours in a deep passionate kiss. Finally, you both break free, and you are both crying and smiling at the same time.

"Oh my god, we are engaged" yells Evan excitedly.

"Yes, sweetheart we are" you respond, still tight in each other's arms you reach up and kiss Evan again. "I love you Evan so much" you whisper.

"I love you too Tori, more than you know. Thank you for saying yes."

As the excitement of the engagement starts to wind down you both make your way to the lounge, as you both sit together, Evan holds you tightly in his arms and then says "Sweetheart, please accept this ring" as he places a huge diamond ring on your ring finger.

"It is beautiful Evan, I love it" you say as you stare mesmerised at the ring on your finger.

"Tori, I know we have just become engaged, but I would like us to be married before our little boy comes into the world."

"Oh really, will we have time to plan everything, I will be a very pregnant bride" you respond thinking.

"Do not worry about that, I have taken the liberty of designing a dress for you, you will be beautiful sweetheart as always" says Evan.

"You have designed a dress really; you know the saying it is bad luck for the groom to see the wedding dress before the wedding" you joke.

"Yes, I have heard that saying, that is why I have designed two for you. You can choose one of them, do not tell me which one, that way it will still be a surprise – so no bad luck" Evan says.

"Oh wow, you really have thought of everything haven't you sweetheart, so when do I get to see these dresses?" you ask smiling.

"Funny you should ask that" Evan says, "I actually have the designs here for you to see and choose."

"Really you have the dresses here, well go get them quick" you order laughing.

"Ok, Ok one second let me go and get them" chuckles Evan as he stands to go and get the designs from his portfolio.

As Evan goes to get the designs your mind wanders back to the day a few days ago when you saw Evan working busily on a design, but he did not want to show you, you wonder if he was working on a design for your wedding dress. Evan excitedly returns with the two designs. You excitedly take them. The first one is a striking white off the shoulder design with a full skirt with central bow design.

The second one is a stunning ivory design, with a detailed lace bodice and long lace sleeves with a long flowing skirt which would complement your growing baby bump.

You fall in love instantly with both of these designs and have trouble picking a favourite. You see Evan anxiously watching you as you study each design, trying to read your reaction. You turn to Evan smiling "Oh Evan these are both beautiful, absolutely stunning, I love them both so much, I cannot decide which one I would want."

Evan feels relieved, "I am so happy you love them, I worked really hard on them. I wanted them to be perfect for you."

"I can see that sweetheart, they are incredible" you reply.

"Now as I said, do not tell me which one you chose, just tell Helen which one you decide on, she knows all about it and will bring the design to life" instructs Evan.

"Oh, Evan as I said before, you really have thought of everything haven't you." You respond with a chuckle.

"Absolutely my love, I have thought about nothing else since you asked me to be the father of your baby."

"I will definitely think about which dress to go with and let Helen know straight away."

"Excellent, I cannot wait to see which one you choose. I know you will be exquisite in which ever one you choose my darling" says Evan as he leans in and kisses you.

Just then you feel a sensation you have not felt before, you jump slightly "Ooh, I think our boy is excited we are getting married, he has just jumped for joy" you say as you reach for Evan's hand and place it on your tummy so he can feel it too.

"Oh, my goodness, that is incredible" your son kicks against Evan's hand. "Oh wow, does that hurt?" he asks.

"No, it is just a little flutter, it means he is happy and growing well."

You both spend the next few minutes in silence enjoying the baby's movements until he settles.

The next morning when you wake up as you stretch out, you smile widely as you see the magnificent engagement ring on your finger. The memories of the amazing proposal flood back, you are so happy, despite the drama with Jasper, knowing you have Evan by your side gives you the strength to face anything. Evan is still sound asleep, and you cannot wait to tell Lexie the news. You gently climb out of bed so as not to disturb Evan and head to the lounge to call Lexie.

Lexie answers, "Hey lovely lady, what is going on this early in the morning?"

You realise it is about 6:45am "Oh Lexie, sorry to call so early lovely, but I am so excited, I am engaged" you respond excitably.

There is silence on the other end of the phone for a moment and then Lexie screams "What? What did you say?"

"I am engaged to be married; Evan proposed last night."

"Oh wow, that is fantastic news lovely, congratulations I am so excited for you, you have to tell me everything" says Lexie excitedly.

You begin to tell her about how Evan prepared a special roast dinner and then how he got down on one knee and made the heartfelt proposal.

"Oohh that is so beautiful" replies Lexie.

You then explain to her how Evan wishes to get married as soon as possible before the baby arrives and how he has already designed a wedding dress for you to choose.

"I am speechless Tori, that is so romantic, he has really thought of everything, so which dress do you think you will choose" she asks.

"Well, Lexie, they are both absolutely gorgeous, but I really love the ivory one with the full flowing skirt and beautifully decorated lace bodice and sleeves."

"It sounds divine Tori; I cannot wait to see it. So, have you set a date? There is a lot to do, especially before your baby arrives."

"No, we have not set a date yet, but we do want it to be soon, I would prefer to be married before my baby bump becomes really huge" you laugh.

"Yeah, I understand for sure, you want to be comfortable on your special wedding day to."

"Exactly Lexie, that is true" you pause for a moment, "Lexie I have a very important question to ask you, will you be my bridesmaid?"

Lexie pauses momentarily and then squeals down the phone, "Of course Tori, I would be honoured."

You both laugh "Thank you Lexie, that means so much to me, you know I love you like you were my very own sister; I could not think of or want anyone else standing beside me."

"Oh Tori, I feel the same way about you my lovely, you are going to make me cry now" Lexie sniffs in reply.

Just then you hear the ensuite door close, "Ooh I think Evan has just woken up, I will catch up with you soon."

"No worries, I have to go and get ready for work now, I am so excited for you, you have made my day" replies Lexie.

You finish up your phone call just as Evan appears in the room still rubbing sleep from his eyes.

"Good morning my beautiful fiancé, what are you doing out here?" he asks as he plants a kiss on your lips and slides down next to you.

"Good morning fiancé, I was just on the phone to Lexie" you respond with a smile.

Evan smiles, "How is she? Did you tell her our news?"

"Yes, I certainly did, she is so excited for us, she is going to be my bridesmaid."

"Oh, that is great news, that reminds me, I need to organise my best man, I think I will ask my brother, Adam."

"Oh, that is great, when will you tell your family?" you ask almost nervously, as you have not met them before.

"I think we should head up to see them this weekend, what do you think?"

"Ok, that is fast, yes that should be fine."

"Great, I will give mum a call now and set it up" says Evan as he reaches for his phone. As he is about to dial the number, he notices you have an anxious look on your face. "Hey darling, is everything Ok?" he asks.

"Yes, I guess I am just a bit nervous to meet you family is all."

Evan puts his arm around you. "Do not be nervous, they will love you as much as I do."

"I hope so Evan, I am just anxious what they will think about the baby and the fact that I am your boss and …."

Evan put his finger to your lips "Sweetheart, you have nothing to worry about, they are great people, and believe me, Mum and Dad will be over the moon to be a grandparents for sure."

You smile back at him, trying to ease the nerves you feel.

Evan finishes his phone call to his mum and turns to smile at you, "There all done, we are heading there for lunch on Saturday, Adam will be there also. Now my love, we need to discuss a wedding date soon don't you think, I know mum will want all the details."

"Yes, for sure, time certainly is going fast" you respond as you caress your baby bump.

Evan thinks for a moment, "Well our son is due in about five months, How do you feel about getting married in six weeks? The 30th October?"

"Six weeks, do you think that will be time to organise everything" you ask concerned. "There is a lot to do?"

"Well really there is not too much to do really, when you decide on the dress, that is taken care of, we have our bridal party organised, I have a good friend of the family that is a celebrant, so I will see if she is available, it will just be a venue and catering."

"I guess so" you respond, you stop and think "Hey why don't we have the ceremony here? there is plenty of room, and somehow, it will feel like my grandma is here to share in the day as this was her house."

"Tori, that would be awesome, I think that will be a great idea."

You and Evan both kiss to seal the deal, "Well that is sorted, leave the decorations and food up to me, I will organise everything my love" Evan says with a smile.

"Are you sure you don't need any help?" you ask.

"No, you just relax and take care of looking after our growing baby, I will sort everything out."

You kiss Evan, pulling him close, and whisper to him "Thank you so much sweetheart, you are amazing, what did I do to deserve such a wonderful man."

"You are the amazing one sweetheart, this is going to be best wedding ever, you wait and see" Evan responds clapping his hands.

You both spend the rest of the day chatting about wedding ideas, with Evan making lots of notes of things to follow up and organise.

The next day you head back into the office and make your way to Helen's office straight away. As if on cue, she seems to know exactly why you have come in to see her and unable to hide her excitement, throws her arms around you and hugs you tight. "Congratulations Tori, Evan told me his plan, I am so excited for you, now I am busting with anticipation, tell me which dress you chose."

"Oh, thank you Helen, I am so excited myself, I have chosen a dress" you pause to add to the excitement, "I have chosen the ivory dress with full skirt and lace bodice and sleeves."

Helen claps her hands excitedly, "I loved that one too, excellent choice, we will get to work on it straight away, I am so excited. Oh, have you and Evan set a date yet?."

"Well yes Helen we have, we have decided to get married in six weeks, on the 30th October. Is that enough time for you to make the dress?" you ask.

"Fantastic, Tori, not a problem at all, this will be my priority," replies Helen smiling.

"Great, thank you so much Helen, you are a legend."

"My pleasure Tori, this is wonderful news, now I will need to take some measurements now, to make a start, do you have time now?" Helen asks as she reaches for her measuring tape.

"Yes, let's do it" you reply excitedly.

Helen starts making the necessary measurements, "Now Tori, when I make the dress, I will make allowance for any adjustments that may need to be made, for baby boy."

"Yes, that would be great" you respond, "He certainly is growing fast."

CHAPTER 14

*T*he day has arrived when you are to meet Evan's family, you are both in the car taking the two-hour trip to the small country town where Evan's family live. You cannot help being filled with feelings of nervousness, anticipation and excitement. Evan, as always, senses your feelings and gently squeezes your leg and smiles, "It will be great sweetheart, I am so excited for you to meet my family."

You smile back at Evan, "I am excited too."

A few minutes later, Evan takes the turn down a lovely winding track and pulls up to a set of majestic gates. He enters the automatic code and the gates open, and you both follow a long windy tree-lined driveway. Eventually the most elaborate house you have ever seen comes into view. Your breath is taken away by the sight of the two-storey white homestead with bright blue shutters and a sprawling veranda encompassing the exterior.

As you pull up and get out of the car two collie dogs come rushing towards you, tails wagging and eagerly awaiting pats and attention. You lean down to cuddle them, and Evan enthusiastically greets the dogs, "Hey Zoe and Buddy, I have missed you both," their tails wag with excitement as they are unable to contain their excitement and jump up and kiss Evan. Just then you hear the front door and look up to see two people rushing out down the stairs arms outstretched "Oh Evan, come here, it is so great to see you, let me look at you" says the lady as she pulls Evan in for a big hug.

"Hi mum, it is so great to see you too" Evan responds.

The gentleman accompanying Evan's mother grabs Evan's hand and pulls him in for a hug also, "Hey son, great to see you."

"Hey Dad, how are you going?" Evan asks smiling.

"We are doing really well, so excited you are both here, Adam will be along in a little bit" says Evan's mum and then her eyes meet yours. "This must be Tori, I am so excited to meet the beautiful lady that has stolen my little boy's heart, come here" she says as she pulls you in for a kiss on the cheek and heartfelt cuddle.

"That is so lovely to say, I am so excited to meet you too" you respond.

Evan's Dad, turns to you and pulls you in for a hug and kiss on the cheek also, "Hello sweetheart, welcome, so pleased to meet you, Evan has told us so much about you, you are even more beautiful than Evan told us."

"Dad stop" says Evan smiling. "Tori, this is my Dad Xavier and my Mum Vivian, Mum Dad as you have worked out this is the love of my life Tori,"

"Fantastic, you must be tired after your long drive, come in and take a seat, and have something to eat" says Vivian as she ushers you both inside.

"Thank you, your home is truly beautiful" you respond.

"Thank you Tori, it has been a labour of love our whole married life, nearly 35 years, it was a bit run-down when we purchased it, and we have lovingly restored it." says Xavier as he smiles widely gesturing around the lounge room.

Before sitting in the lounge, you try to whisper quietly to Evan, "Babe, where is the bathroom, baby boy is really pressing on my bladder today!"

Evan smiles but before he can answer, Vivian interrupts, "Sweetheart, come this way, you must be uncomfortable, I remember, what it was like when I was pregnant with Evan here, he loved bouncing on my bladder all day every day, thinking it was a trampoline for him in there."

"Mum, really" says Evan laughing with embarrassment.

You follow Vivian down the hall to restroom, "Here sweetie, just in there, I cannot begin to tell you how excited I am to have you here" she says as she gestures to the restroom and squeezes your arm smiling.

After freshening up you return to the lounge and take your seat next to Evan on the couch. Vivian looks at you, "Tori, tell us about yourself, Evan has told us a lot, but we want to know everything about you."

You look at Evan and he smiles, "Well as you may know, my brother and I were raised by our grandmother after our parents were killed in a car crash."

"That is so sad Tori, we are so sorry to hear that" says Xavier.

"Yes it was hard, but our grandmother was amazing, she built McIntyre Fashions from humble beginnings as a home-based business from our kitchen table to what it is today. She was an amazing mentor to me."

"She does sound like an amazing lady; we want to pass on our condolences for her passing several months ago."

"Thank you, that is very much appreciated" you respond.

Vivian asks excitedly, "Please tell us about our grandson?."

"Well, I do not know exactly what Evan has told you, but in her will, Grandma wanted to ensure succession for the business and set the extraordinary requirement that in order for me to inherit full control of McIntyre fashions, I would be required to produce a biological heir within twelve months. As you can imagine, that was a surprise and I was not in a relationship at that time, so I considered an anonymous sperm donor, but then your son Evan walked by my office and the crazy thought came into my head, to ask him to be the father of my child."

"Oh, so you were in love with Evan from the beginning?" Vivian asks.

You look at Evan and you try to think of a response. "Mum, it doesn't matter, what matters is that we are in love now and we are so happy to be having this beautiful special little boy" say Evan firmly.

"Evan, I am just wanting to get to know Tori and understand how the events happened is all" Vivian responds defiantly.

"Vivian, I will be honest, I have always found Evan attractive for sure, but if you were asking me if I was in love with Evan right from the beginning, well No, I was not then, but the more time I have spent with Evan and sharing the pregnancy, my feelings for him have definitely changed, and he is truly a wonderful man in every way, I could not imagine my life without him at all, I do love him now with all my heart".

Evan kisses you on the cheek, you turn to Vivian and Xavier and are relieved to see them both smiling after your confession. "Well Tori, it does warm our heart to hear how strongly you feel for our son. We can see how happy he is with you and the impending arrival of our grandson." says Vivian.

You smile in response.

You continue to chat about the fashion business and Blaze designs, not yet broaching the topic of Jasper.

You all hear another car door shut, "Oh that must be Adam" says Xavier as he stands to greet his eldest son. You sit with Evan holding his hand waiting for Adam to enter, seconds later, Xavier returns with a tall slightly older version of Evan, closely followed by a petite blonde lady holding a toddler with tightly curled dark hair with a bright pink bow. Vivian jumps up and hugs Adam and the accompanying lady and quickly grabs the little toddler from her mother's arms. "Come to Granny, my precious Yasmin." coos Vivian as she swings the toddler around in the air, the little girl squealing with excitement.

Adam and his partner make their way over to you and Evan who are now standing, Adam reaches out his hand to his brother, "Hey Bro, how are you going? Great to see you" he says as he pulls Evan in and gives him a slap on the back."

194

"Hey Adam, great to see you too" replies Evan. Evan leans in and plants a kiss on the cheek of the lady standing next to Adam. "Hey Paige, how are you going, great to see you and little Yasmin."

"Great to see you too Evan" replies Paige and then she turns her focus to you. "Hello there, you must be Tori, my name is Paige, I am Adam's wife, and this bundle of trouble is little Yasmin" she replies as points towards the toddler still in Vivian's strong grip.

"Adam, Paige, and baby Yasmin, it is a pleasure to meet you all" you respond as you stand next to Evan.

Adam turns to face you, "Pleasure to meet you Tori, it is so great to meet the lady that has tamed my baby brother" he says as he pulls you in for a hug and kiss on the cheek.

You cannot help but feel so happy, to be welcomed so wonderfully by Evan's family.

"Great, now everyone is here, let's get ready to eat, boys, come and help you old man with the BBQ and we will let these women catch up and have a good old girly chin wag" says Xavier as he leads the way out the back to the BBQ via the kitchen.

Evan turns to you and whispers "Are you Ok? Have fun with mum and Paige, you will be fine, love you" and then plants a kiss on your lips.

You take a deep breath and nod in agreement and then watch him as he heads out the back with Adam and Xavier.

"Come on Tori, come into the kitchen while the men are out there burning the meat" laughs Vivian "It really is an excuse for them to drink and talk cars, tools and sport."

You nod your head and follow Vivian and Paige into the kitchen.

"So, Paige how old is little Yasmin" you ask.

"She is nearly 12 months old and has just started to find her feet, Adam and I will be in trouble soon, nothing will be safe" smiles Paige. "By the way congratulations on your pregnancy, it is a really exciting time.

Truthfully I never thought Evan would settle down, his fashion career was always his dream, no time for ladies."

"Oh really, I did not know that about him, I suspected he would have had lots of partners" you reply.

"Nope, there has been none, not since I have known him, and Adam and I have been together for the past six years coming up next month."

You smile and your heart feels even more strongly for Evan.

You spend the next hour or so with Paige and Vivian, preparing salads and other lunch accompaniments chatting about pregnancy, and Adam and Evan as youngsters growing up, you feel so comfortable and happy. The boys come back in with a large plate of cooked meat that looks and smells delicious. Evan makes his way over to you, "Everything good?" he asks.

"Yes sweetheart, everything is great" you respond smiling, giving him a kiss.

"Aww that is so sweet" says Vivian, as she watches the both of you. "Quick everyone help yourself before the meat gets cold."

You all pile up your plates with meat and salad and make your way to the large dining table and enjoy the food and endless amounts of laughter and chatter.

The time finally comes for Evan to break the news of your engagement, he whispers to you "Ready? Let's tell them all now."

You nod in agreement, Evan clears his throat, "Hey everyone, Tori and I have an announcement to make."

The table turns silent, and focuses on Evan, even baby Yasmin stops playing in her highchair and looks over intently at Evan.

"Well, everyone, I want to tell you that Tori has made me the happiest man alive, not only are we having this special little boy in a few months, but this week she has agreed to become my wife."

Everyone erupts with cheers and squeals, and rush over to you both and hug and kiss you both.

"Son that is great news, we are so excited to welcome Tori into our family, hope we have not scared you off today" laughs Xavier.

"Not all Xavier, it has been so much fun being here today, I have loved meeting you all, you all have made me feel so welcome."

"That is great news darling welcome to our family Tori, it is such exciting news, we have so much to plan" says Vivian as she reaches for a pen and paper to begin making a list.

"Mum, Mum slow down, everything is under control, Tori and I have planned everything" says Evan.

"Oh, really, there must be something I can do, my baby boy is getting married, I have to do something" says Vivian almost disappointed that there is nothing for her to do.

Sensing Vivian's disappointment, you think for a minute, well there is one thing I need help with" you say.

Vivian's eyes light up, "Really what do you need?"

"I need help with flowers and party favours, are you able to help us with that?"

"Absolutely, leave it with me, now I need details, where and when is it?" replies Vivian clapping her hands together with excitement.

"We are getting married in 6 weeks at our home, in the gardens" says Evan,

"Oh, that sounds beautiful, anything I can help with?" asks Paige.

"You can help Vivian and I am sure I will need lots of help to get ready on the big day" you reply.

"For sure, we will be honoured" both Vivian and Paige respond.

"Now, there is the matter of my best man I need to address" says Evan as he looks over at Adam. "Hey Bro, will you do me the honour of being my best man."

Adam's face erupts with a huge smile, "Absolutely Bro."

"Excellent, that is all sorted" Evan says triumphantly. The rest of the afternoon is spent discussing the wedding plans and then it is time to head home.

As you pull out of side road back on to the main road, Evan turns to you, gently squeezes your knee, "So Darling, that went really well, don't you think?"

"Yes, Sweetheart, your family are amazing, I had such a wonderful time, thank you so much for bringing me today" you respond smiling.

"They loved you too, I knew that they would" replies Evan.

You smile to yourself, feeling content with the events of the day, and before long the gentle motion of the car ride home sends you to sleep.

CHAPTER 15

A few days later, you and Evan are busily working in your office and also finalising plans for the upcoming wedding, when your phone suddenly rings and it is Mario.

"Hi Mario, how are you going?" you ask.

"Hi Tori, I am very well, I have to meet with you as soon as possible, I have uncovered some more information about Jasper in the last couple of days that I really must share with you as soon as possible" replies Mario almost frantically.

"Ok, certainly, do you want to meet at that same coffee shop again?" you ask as you stare at Evan in surprise.

"Yes, that will be great, can you meet me there in say thirty minutes?"

"Yes Mario, we will be there, not a problem, see you then."

You hang up the phone and turn to Evan, "Mario needs to see us immediately, he has uncovered more news on Jasper, we need to leave now."

"Ok, let's go" says Evan as he grabs the car keys and you both head to the elevator. As you pass by Rene, you mention briefly, "Rene, sorry for the short notice, Evan and I have to head out briefly, we will be back soon."

"No problem" replies Rene as she watches you enter the elevator.

Once you are in the car, you say to Evan, " I wonder what Mario has found out, it sounded pretty urgent that he meet with us right away."

"Oh well we are nearly there, and we will find out soon enough" replies Evan calmly.

As you and Evan enter the coffee shop you see Mario sitting at the table in the far corner. He notices you enter and acknowledges you. As you reach his table, he shakes both your hands, and you all sit down anxiously awaiting the new that Mario has to share with you.

"Hi guys, thank you for meeting me so quickly, as I mentioned on the phone earlier, I have uncovered some news regarding Jasper which is to say the least quite concerning." says Mario.

"Really that does not sound good" you reply nervously.

Mario continues, "Well as I mentioned in our last meeting, I was going to continue my surveillance of Jasper, well I have been able to uncover the extent of his involvement with the gang 'The Hopper Royals', it would appear that he has gotten himself into some trouble with gambling and as a result he has incurred a large amount of debt, and the Hopper Royals are demanding their money immediately".

"Oh no, are you sure, how do you know this Mario" you ask.

"Well, I have been tapping into his phone conversations, and followed his movements. The gang leaders have issued him a demand to pay up or face some pretty serious implications."

"Like what implications?" Evan asks.

"Well, there has been physical threats made to him and I am sorry to say, they are aware of you Tori and have mentioned you as a potential person of interest to them."

Your eyes widen and you can sense Evan tensing up beside you. "Oh, my goodness, should we go to the police?" Evan asks.

"No, Evan not yet, as no immediate threats have been made against you both, the police will be unable to help you, we need you to just stay vigilant of your surroundings and take all reasonable care to stay as safe as possible."

"Ok we will do that" replies Evan.

"Unfortunately, that is not all the news I have uncovered" continues Mario, " I can now explain to you why your business is now of great concern to Jasper. It appears that he has detailed a scheme to repay his debt to the gang. I have evidence of a phone conversation where Jasper has discussed him gaining ownership of McIntyre Fashions and then selling it with the proceeds going to the gang to repay his debt."

You gasp in shock, "No No he cannot do that, we have to stop him."

Mario's face darkens "I have an idea which may work to save the company and also help Jasper in the process."

You and Evan look at Mario puzzled.

Mario continues "I have an associate within the police force who has been investigating the dealings of the Hopper Royals gang. If we can persuade Jasper to assist the police by working with them to bring this gang down, the police will look favourably on his case."

After a pause you ask, "You want Jasper to be a police informant?"

"Yes, that is what I am saying" responds Mario.

"How do you suggest we persuade Jasper to assist the police?" asks Evan.

"I know under the circumstances, this may be a big ask, but the only way is for you to talk to him and persuade him to help the police and ultimately himself" replies Mario.

"Jasper and my current relationship is tense at best at the moment, why do you think he will listen to anything I have to say?" you ask.

"I understand Tori, but you need to convince Jasper that we have evidence against him that links him to the gang, which if provided to the police will put him in prison for quite some time. He needs to understand that his only avenue to be free from jail and the tight grasp of the gang is to assist the police now and put these criminals behind bars."

Evan looks at you, "Look Tori, I really feel that this is our only option to save the company and to save your brother. We can do this; I will be right beside you every step of the way."

You ponder the thought for a moment then take a deep breath, "Alright, I will try, for us, our company and also to help Jasper."

"Good girl, Tori, I will be with you" says Evan as he pulls you in for a hug.

"Ok Mario, so now what do you suggest, how do we start this plan" you ask intently.

"Well Tori, you will need to make contact with Jasper, try to set up a meeting" he notices the engagement ring on your finger, smiling he continues, "You can mention it has something to do with your upcoming wedding, congratulations by the way."

You and Evan both smile, "Thanks Mario, yes we are very excited about the wedding, Ok, I will see if he will meet with me" you reply.

"Good, once you get the meeting, you can advise him about the evidence I have uncovered and that in order to help himself, he needs to cooperate with the police. I will be in close proximity and the police will also be on standby if needed."

Feeling nervous about the requirements, you nod to Mario in agreement, "Ok, I will make contact and set up a meeting with him as soon as possible."

"Thanks Tori, please keep me informed."

With that you all stand and depart the coffee shop. As you return to the car, you say to Evan "I think we should go home and I will call Jasper from there, considering the relationship between Rene and Jasper, I cannot risk her getting wind of our plan here."

"Yes, that is a great point" replies Evan as he turns the car around and begins to head back home. The whole trip you are running scenarios of what you will say to Jasper when you speak to him.

When you arrive home, you pick up the phone to call Jasper, as the phone rings, your heart is beating fast, Evan is right beside you, you feel his unwavering support.

"Hello Tori, to what do I owe this pleasure?" Jasper answers on the other end of the line.

"Hi Jasper, I would like to meet with you please, I have come up with a plan regarding the company that I would like to run past you. How soon can I meet with you?"

There is silence on the other end of the line, "That is interesting, why can't you tell me over the phone or via our lawyers?" he asks.

"Jasper you are my brother, I want to see you in person, why is that a problem?" you respond.

"No of course not, I am just surprised is all" you hear him flick through the pages of a diary, "You are in luck, I am free tomorrow, I have other business to attend to back home, I will meet up with you tomorrow say 2.00pm"

"That sounds great, Ok, come to the house, see you then."

"Ok, see you then" replies Jasper and then he hangs up the phone.

You turn to Evan, relieved, "Well that seemed to be easy, the hard part will be coming tomorrow, I suspect."

Evan nods his head in response, squeezes your hand "We have got this don't worry sweetheart,"

"I hope you are right."

The time arrives for Jasper to arrive, Mario is in position in the back room out of sight, but able to listen in to the discussions about to take place. You have been reassured that the police are positioned out of sight, but close by should they be required to intervene. Just then there is a knock on the door. You and Evan reach for the door, on the other side is Jasper, slightly dishevelled in appearance with a noticeable bruise above his right eye. "Oh, my goodness Jasper, what has happened to you?" you ask as you usher him inside.

"Nothing, I am fine, I had to leave very early this morning, to get here, and it was dark, and I bumped into the bathroom door." Jasper says as he cautiously touches his bruised eye. You watch him as he heads towards the couch and you notice him protect his ribs as he takes a seat, and he tries unconvincingly to hide a slight grimace as he sits.

"Must have been some angry bathroom door" states Evan as you both take a seat across from Jasper.

Jasper looks at you and a small smile appears on his face. Despite what he has put you both through, you feel concern for him, and your motherly instincts kick in "Are you sure you are ok, do you need anything?" you ask concerned.

"No, I am fine, now what do you want to discuss with me in person that you couldn't tell me over the phone" Jasper asks hurriedly.

You try to recall the set speech you had set in your mind, "Well Jasper, we asked you here today to discuss the company and the legal issues that have arisen."

"Ok, go on I am listening" Jasper responds as he takes a shortbread and cup of coffee from the coffee table.

"Well Jasper, I am not going to sugar coat the situation, I am going to come straight to the point, Some information has come to our

212

attention which links you to the gang the Hopper Royals."

Jasper appears to almost choke on his coffee, "What are you talking about?, that is absurd where did you hear that?"

Despite his denial, you know him well enough to know how he behaves when his actions have been caught out. "We know that you owe them a large amount of money and you are only interested in McIntyre fashions so you can sell it and pay them out."

Jasper shakes his head in disbelief, "You think you are so smart; you are so wrong, you cannot prove anything."

"We have proof of text messages, telephone calls and secret meetings" says Evan.

"You are lying, how would you get that, have you had me followed?" exclaims Jasper, he is about to stand in frustration, but the pain in his ribs makes him stay put.

"Yes, Jasper, I am sorry, we have had your monitored, but you left us no choice after what you had done with the legal issues. We had to work out the truth."

Jasper's jaw tightens, he continues to shake his head, looking down he thinks for a moment, "I cannot believe you would do this to me Tori."

"I cannot believe what you were doing to me and Grandma's company, we had to stop you destroying her legacy" you reply. "Jasper, tell us the truth, what is going on please."

Jasper looks at you, and you can see tears forming in his eyes, he tries to fight them, but his efforts are futile. He looks away from you, finally he manages to speak. "Alright Tori, you are right, I am in trouble, I am not proud of it."

You get up and sit down next to him and embrace him "Jasper it is ok, we want to help you."

Jasper falls into your embrace and his tears flow "Tori, I am sorry, I am in so deep, I don't know how to fix it" he sobs.

You hold Jasper, letting him get his emotions out, consoling him as best as you can. After a while you pull away, "Jasper, we have a plan that we believe can help you, it is not going to be easy, but we think it is the best option."

Jasper wipes his eyes and listens to you as you outline the plan to him. "Jasper, you need to go to the police and tell them everything you know about the gang and their activities."

"Tori are you kidding me, no way, they will kill me and you for sure" replies Jasper frantically as he shakes his head.

"Jasper, I know for sure that if you help the police bring down this gang, the police will protect you, I promise."

Jasper asks, "How do you know that?" Just then there is a knock on the door and a police officer is standing on the other side. You let him in "Good afternoon Jasper McIntyre, my name is Senior constable Jones, I have been listening to this conversation and I want to reassure that if you agree to help us bring down this gang, we will look after you and your sister, you have our word on that."

Jasper still unconvinced, tenses up "Constable, I don't know, how can you guarantee our safety not to mention the implications of my involvement with this gang?"

Constable Jones looks at Jasper "We have been trying to get a strong hold on this gang for a very long time, if you agree to tell us everything you know about them, they will be put behind bars for a very long time."

"And what happens to me?" Jasper asks.

"If you co-operate we will quash any criminal case against you, I can assure you of that."

Jasper thinks for a moment, and then finally agrees to assist the police. "Alright, I will help you, I will tell you everything I know."

"Very good, Mr McIntyre, can you please accompany me to the station and make a formal statement?" requests Senior constable Jones.

Jasper nods his head and stands to follow the senior constable to the door, before he leaves he turns to you "Thank you Sis, for helping me, after everything I did to you both, I cannot believe you would do this for me."

"You are my brother Jasper, I love you, now get going and say your piece and get back here afterwards and we can really catch up" you smile as you playfully put a hand on his arm.

"Thank you Tori, by the way congratulations on the baby and the engagement you two" Jasper says smiling.

"Hey, how did you know about the engagement?" you ask.

"Are you kidding, I was nearly blinded by the rock on your finger" Jasper jokes as he follow the police out the door.

As you watch Jasper get into the police car, Evan places his arms around you. "See sweetheart, it has all worked out, it is over now."

"I hope so Evan, I really hope so" you respond as you watch the police car drive away.

You farewell Mario who has been intently listening in the next room, very pleased that his work has been a success, you and Evan try to relax as you wait for Jasper to return from the police station.

Hours and hours pass and finally Jasper returns to the house. He looks extremely tired and pale from what you can only imagine was an intense questioning by the police. You pull him in for a hug, and then show him to the lounge. "Hey Jasper, do you want anything to drink, or eat?" you ask.

"I could definitely go for a beer if you have one" Jasper responds as he flops on the couch and rubs his hands over his face and through his hair and lets out a large audible sigh.

"Absolutely mate, I will get you one" responds Evan as he heads to the kitchen.

As Evan returns and hands the beer to Jasper, you ask "So how did it go?"

After taking a swig of the beer, Jasper says "Well I told them everything I know, the drug deals, the break-ins, the threats against you and me, everything. The police are on their way to make arrests as we speak, it should be over."

"Oh, that is a relief for everyone concerned Jasper, you did the right thing for sure" you reply.

"Oh Tori, I hope so, I hope that they get them all, and this nightmare over the past six months can finally be over, and I can get my life back."

"You will Jasper, you have taken the first step, Evan and I will help you for sure" you say reassuringly.

"Thanks again sis, as I said before, I cannot believe you are helping me, after what I have done to you both, I am truly sorry, I felt I had no other way" says Jasper.

"Do not worry about that now, you are safe now, you are my brother Jasper, I love you and I will always be here for you."

"Thank you, Thank you both of you" Jasper responds smiling.

"Ok, good, now let's have some dinner" you say as you make your way to the kitchen.

You all enjoy a well-deserved dinner and catch up.

"So, tell me how things are going with the baby?" asks Jasper, "I still cannot believe that I am going to be an uncle so soon."

"Everything is going really well, our little boy is growing bigger and stronger every day, so far the pregnancy has been quite smooth, no dramas" you reply.

"Well, no thanks to what I put you both through, about that I am really sorry again, I will speak to my legal team as soon as possible and get them to back off" says Jasper.

"Thank you Jasper, about that, I have been thinking, if you would like, you can have a share of the company, it is Grandma's legacy, it would only be right for us to share it" you say offering an olive branch to Jasper.

"That means a lot Tori, but I do not know the first thing about fashion" replies Jasper laughing.

"Well think about it, it can be part of your new life" says Evan.

Jasper smiles and nods his head and is unable to hide a yawn.

"You are really tired, stay here tonight in the spare room it is all made up ready for you" you say.

"Thanks Tori, I am pretty wiped out, been a huge day" responds Jasper as he stands up "Good night, we will chat in the morning."

"Good night" and with that you an Evan clean up and then retire for the night yourselves. As you climb into bed, Evan encompasses you in his strong arms, and you begin to feel relief that things have improved with Jasper and the nightmare of the legal issues are nearly over before you know it you fall asleep.

The next morning when you wake up, Jasper is already up and is on his phone when you and Evan enter the kitchen. You cannot help listening to his conversation and realise that he is speaking to the police. "Thank you constable, I am so relieved that you have been able to find them all and they are now in custody, thank you for updating me" says Jasper as he turns around and notices you and Evan, smiling he acknowledges you both. He finishes the phone call and turns to you both, "It's over, that was the police, they have got them all" Jasper says smiling.

"Oh, that is great news Jasper" you respond.

You all enjoy breakfast together, Jasper stretches "Well this has been good, but I better get going and get back home, got a long drive today."

"Of course, I am so glad that we have been able to sort things out, Jasper I do have a very important question to ask you before you go please" you ask nervously.

"Of course, Tori, what do want to ask me" asks Jasper.

"Well as you know, Evan and I are getting married in just under six weeks now, now that we have reconciled our differences, would you please do me the honour of walking me down the aisle at the wedding?"

Jasper's eyes widen with surprise and then his face erupts in a huge smile, "Oh my goodness, yes Tori, that would mean so much to me, thank you so much, of course I will do that" says Jasper as he pulls you in for a big hug.

You feel relief take over as you return the hug, Evan comes closer and pats you both on the back.

You farewell Jasper and promise to keep in touch with each other more regularly and watch him disappear out the drive.

CHAPTER 16

The next six weeks fly by in a blur and before you know it, your wedding day has arrived. You have spent the night at Lexie's apartment so as to fulfill the old superstition of not seeing the groom before the wedding. Lexie and some of your fellow female work colleagues held an impromptu hens night for you last night, they took you out to a special dinner followed by a live comedy show. You felt so special and had a wonderful time with the girls The girls in solidarity with you did not drink any alcohol and proved that you do not necessarily need alcohol to have a wonderful evening. As you awake in Lexie's spare room the magnitude of the day ahead dawns on you, you are filled with feelings of pre wedding nerves but most of all excitement. The image of Evan waiting for you at the end of the wedding aisle and declaring your love for each other brings a warm smile to your face. A gentle knock on the door stirs you from your thoughts.

You hear Lexie quietly ask from the other side of the door "Good morning Tori, are you awake?"

"Yes Lexie, come in?"

The door opens and Lexie comes bounding in with her usual excitement. "Good morning lovely, are you ready to marry your Prince Charming today?" she asks.

Your face lights up with a huge smiling and you almost scream with excitement "Yes, Yes I cannot wait to marry Evan today" you embrace Lexie and share a deep hug.

"Alright then, we have lots to do, let's start with breakfast" says Lexie as she gently pulls you out of bed towards the kitchen.

As you reach the kitchen you are met with a delicious spread of toast, condiments, croissants, muffins, eggs and bacon. "Oh, wow Lexie, this is amazing" you say as you peruse the assortment. As you are about to make your selection, there is a knock at the door, Lexie rushes to open the door and you hear the familiar voice of Jasper. "Morning Lexie, I assume that Tori is here?"

"Hey Jasper, yes I am come in" you yell from the kitchen.

As Jasper enters the kitchen you smile, "Just in time brother, help yourself to some breakfast."

"Good morning Sis are you ready for your special day?" he asks as he plants a kiss on your cheek before grabbing a plate, "Oh wow, what do we have here?."

"Hey Bro, yes I am so excited for today" you respond.

The three of you make your selections and sit together at the table chatting about the day ahead. Since reporting the crimes of the gang to the police, Jasper has been informed that there will be a court case in approximately a month's time where it is highly probable that all the gang members will be sentenced to extensive time in prison for their crimes, and as promised, he has had all his involvement with the gang quashed by the police. You can see the relief in his eyes, and you are so thankful that you have your brother here with you again to share this day.

Shortly after breakfast, the hair and makeup team arrive. "Hey, I think that is my cue to leave" jokes Jasper, "I will be back later ok." He gives you and Lexie a kiss on the cheek and heads for the door.

The next hour or two is spent being fussed over and being transformed ready for your wedding. You both have decided to wear your hair down but gently curled. The time has come for putting on your wedding gown. As promised Helen had it finished well ahead of time and you had your final fitting just this week and after a couple of slight alterations for growing baby boy, the dress is now ready to see in its entirety for the first time. As you unzip the garment bag, your breath is taken away, the dress is even more stunning in real life than the drawings and what you have seen during its creation. You tell yourself not to cry so as not to mess up your freshly applied make-up. Just as you pull the dress out of the garment bag, Lexie comes into the room, "Oh my goodness Tori, that is amazing, you are going to be absolutely stunning."

You turn to Lexie, "it is amazing isn't it, help me put it on."

Once it is on, you turn to look at yourself in the full-length mirror and the dress fits perfectly, you feel like a princess. Lexie adjusts the dress perfectly for you and helps you into your veil.

"Tori, you are truly stunning, Evan is going to flip out when he sees you in this" says Lexie.

"Thank you Lexie, you look amazing too" you reply. Not only did Evan design your wedding dress, but he also designed the bridesmaid dress for Lexie, an amazing off the shoulder ruby red dress with a stunning lace bodice and body-hugging skirt.

Shortly after Jasper returns looking very handsome in his dark tuxedo. When he sees you, he gasps "Tori you are beautiful."

"Thank you, hey you don't scrub up too bad yourself" you reply laughing.

The time has arrived to head back to the house for the ceremony, you make your way outside to get into the limousine waiting out the front, but before you get in a little girl comes rushing up to you with a little flower she has pulled from her own garden, as she hands it to you she says "Here miss, please take this, you look beautiful"

"Thank you so much sweetie, I will put it pride of place in my bouquet" you say so much as you gently push the flower into your bouquet. The little girl squeals with excitement and runs back to her mother who waves at you smiling. You wave back and then you all enter the limousine for the drive back to the house.

As you pull up outside your home, you feel remarkably calm, you are excited about the ceremony and marrying the love of your life.

As you enter the house and make your way out to the garden outside, Vivian and Xavier appear.

"Hello Tori, we just wanted to see you before you go inside, you look stunning, can you please accept this necklace to wear today?" asks Vivian as she places an exquisite pearl necklace in your hand. "It was my mother's, and I would love for you to have it."

"Oh, Vivian it is beautiful, are you sure?" you ask.

"Absolutely Darling, you are my daughter in law now, I want you to have it."

"Thank you so much Vivian, would you mind putting it on me?" you ask.

"Absolutely dear" she says as she carefully places it around your neck and fastens the clasp. She gently kisses your cheek, "Welcome to the family Darling" she says as she heads for her seat.

Xavier grabs your hand and gently squeezes it, "Welcome to the family Tori, you look magnificent."

"Thank you so much" you reply, and Xavier heads to join his wife at the front of the crowd.

The wedding music begins, and you prepare to walk down the aisle to see Evan.

Lexie leads the way. Jasper turns to you and winks "Are you ready?" he asks.

You nod smiling in reply and start the walk down the aisle. Everyone stands and turns to watch you, their faces erupting in smiles as they see you. Then your eyes meet the familiar eyes of Evan, a feeling of complete calm and peace comes over you, you want to run straight to him but you know you have to stay composed, you do however quicken the pace slightly which takes Jasper a little by surprise, he looks down at you smiling and then meets your pace and before you know it you are at the end and standing beside Evan, who is beaming from ear to ear. you notice tears welling up in his eyes as he whispers to you, "You look magnificent my love."

You whisper back to him "So do you darling."

Everyone takes their seats, and the celebrant prepares to begin the ceremony. You pass your bouquet to Lexie and turn to face Evan, holding his hands tightly.

The celebrant begins "Welcome everyone, we are here on this stunning day to witness the joining of Tori McIntyre and Evan Thomas in holy matrimony."

Despite being surrounded by many people you can only focus on Evan in front of you. The time arrives for your vows which you have each written yourselves.

Evan begins "Tori, my darling, when I first met you when I first started working at McIntyre fashions, I knew then and told myself this is the lady I am going to marry, and eighteen months later, here we are. You have made me the happiest man in the world. You are amazing, strong, funny and not to mention incredibly hot, I will spend every day of the rest of my life making you the happiest woman in the world. We have already faced a lot together, and I cannot wait to see what our future holds as we welcome our little boy very soon. I love you Tori."

It is now your turn, you blink away the tears stinging at your eyes "My darling Evan, although it may have taken me a little longer than you to see our destiny, I see now what a wonderful caring loving man you are. You came to me at a difficult time in my life and helped me and my love for you grew from that point and is now fiercely strong. You have supported me through it all and you have given me two of the most amazingly special things, this beautiful little boy and the love of a wonderful partner to share my life with me for ever. I love you so much Evan."

The celebrant now retrieves the rings from Adam, "We have now listened to the lovely wedding vows, it is now time to exchange rings" says the celebrant.

Evan takes the ring and places it on your finger "Tori, please accept this ring as a symbol of my never-ending love for you."

You now take the ring and place it on Evan's finger, "Evan, please accept this ring as a symbol of my never-ending love for you."

"Wonderful" says the celebrant smiling, "We have all witnessed the sharing of those lovely vows and the giving and receiving of the precious wedding rings, it is now my extreme pleasure to invite Evan to seal this wedding by kissing his new wife Tori."

Evan smiles widely as he carefully lifts your veil and places his hands on either side of your face and leans in and envelops your mouth entirely with his in a deep passionate kiss. You wrap your arms around his neck and reciprocate the passion. You both hear loud cheers and clapping of hands from your guests which brings you back to reality quickly. Reluctantly you both break free from your kiss and turn to face your adoring friends and family.

Your celebrant manages to gain control of the crowd long enough to say, " It is with my absolute pleasure to present to you Mr and Mrs Evan Thomas." The crowd erupt with cheers and clapping again as you and Evan join hands and proceed to walk back down the aisle as a newly married couple.

The rest of the night is spent enjoying a delicious meal and celebrating with friends and family. The time in the night arrives when the party ends and after thanking and farewelling all your guests, it is time for you and your new husband to retire for the evening. Hand in hand you both make your way to your bedroom and when you open the door you are both surprised to see that your bedroom has been transformed into a magical bridal suite, with white silky linen on the bed, a luxurious white duvet sprinkled with dozens of red rose petals. There is non-alcoholic cider chilling in the corner and on the bedside table is a plate of your favourite milk crème chocolates. "Oh, my goodness, did you do this?" you ask Evan.

"No way, not guilty, it was not me" Evan replies, he is in as much surprise as you as he looks around the room.

"I wonder who did this? You ask, "I bet it was "Lexie, Paige and your mum, now that I think of it, they all did disappear for a little while earlier."

"It sounds like something Mum and Paige would definitely be into" laughs Evan as he picks up one of the chocolates to feed to you.

"Oh wow, my favourite" you reply as you savour the chocolate.

Evan then pours you a glass of the non-alcoholic cider and passes it to you. "To my beautiful wife"

"Thank you my darling husband" you reply, and you both take a sip together.

As you sit on the bed, you sigh happily, "Today was just perfect."

"It certainly was my darling, now we are together for ever" he responds kissing you again.

Evan then begins to caress your shoulder as he moves his arms behind you to begin to unzip the dress, as he does so he whispers to you. "I am so glad that you chose this dress, I was hoping you would, it was my favourite and as I suspected you looked absolutely exquisite in it," he then begins to pepper your neck with kisses.

"The dress was perfect, you are perfect, today was perfect, I could not be happier" you say as your place your hands underneath Evan's suit jacket and begin to caress his strong abs which sends feeling of pleasure rush through your body.

Before you know it, you and Evan are both naked and Evan gently picks you up and places you on the bed amongst the dozens of petals and crashes his lips on to yours. Your hands travel down his body until they meet his exposed length, which is now hard to the touch, you grab it in your hands and gently stroke it feeling it become firmer with each stroke of your hand. Evan grabs your breasts squeezing them between his fingers, he then moves his mouth over your aroused nipples gently squeezing them in his mouth. You gasp at his touch and begin to quicken the strokes on his length causing him to moan and breathe deeply in response. His hands travel down and stop at your every expanding baby bump where he gently caresses every inch. His lips move down and pepper your stomach with kisses as his hands move in between your legs to your sweet spot where his touch fills your body with a multitude of pleasure. Placing your hands on his face, you turn him to face you, "Make love to me now darling, I want to feel you inside of me" you order.

Evan responds obediently and you feel him penetrate you and fill you with his manhood. You both begin to move your hips in unison, your breathes becoming deeper and more rapid with each thrust. Moans of ecstasy fill the room as you both reach your climax almost simultaneously. You both lay next to each other, still caressing each other intimately as you both catch your breath. Shortly after, the huge events of the day catch up with you both and sleep takes over.

The next morning, Evan wakes you up with a deep kiss and hug. "Good morning, my wife, we need to get going on our honeymoon."

Stretching you force your eyes open and grimace and try to pull the covers back up over your head.

"No, come on sweetheart, we have to get ready to go" urges Evan as he reaches under the covers to tickle you.

"All right, All right, I will get up" your shriek as you try to avoid Evan's tickles.

"Good, let's shower and get ready to go."

You reluctantly climb out of bed, stretching more as you make your way to the bathroom. As you are entering your final trimester of pregnancy, you have decided to take a road trip for your honeymoon and avoid flying. You both have decided to travel up to a cottage in the countryside which Evan's parents own.

An hour later you are both in the car packed ready to set off, Evans holds your hand as he drives out of the drive. You pass by and stop at some amazing lookouts and small country towns as you travel to your destination.

After several hours, Evan finally pulls up outside a lovely little cottage, with a beautiful English garden theme. "Oh, Evan this is beautiful, I feel like I am in the English countryside."

"Yes Mum and Dad have spent a lot of time on this. Mum loves the quaint English villages, and it has been her mission to recreate her own little English country cottage here."

You both make your way inside and the cottage is even more beautiful on the inside as on the outside. There is a gorgeous fireplace in the corner, lovely hardwood flooring and striking beams on the ceiling. The furniture is antique and looks both exquisite and comfortable at the same time. You and Evan take a seat on the plush sofa in front of the fireplace. "This is amazing Evan; I love it here."

Evan smiles "Yes, Mum and Dad have spent a lot of time and money sourcing this items, mum definitely has a flair for interior design."

"That she certainly does" you reply in amazement, as you gaze around at all the beautiful items adorning the walls and cabinets around the room. As the late afternoon air begins to fall, Evan decides to light the fire and soon the room is filled with the gorgeous glow of the open fire. As you both sit by the fire, you enjoy a non-alcoholic drink and snack on cheese and crackers. Before long, the last of the day's sun disappears and you both snuggle together with only the glow of the fire lighting the room. "Did you want some dinner?" Evan asks.

"No not really, I feel we have been snacking all day, unless you want something" you reply.

"No, I have everything I need right here" Evan responds kissing you on the forehead as

241

he pulls you in closer under the blanket on the couch.

You spend the next few hours just snuggled together, reminiscing about the wedding until you can no longer keep your eyes open and resting your head on Evan's chest you fall asleep.

CHAPTER 17

*T*he next day you awake to a beautiful crisp morning, the sun is beginning to shine, there is dew on the trees outside and birds are happily chirping. You turn to face Evan and kiss him on the lips, he awakes with a start and then begins to smile back at you as he slowly opens his eyes for the day. "Good morning my husband, what are we going to do today" you ask excitedly.

Stretching his arms out around you he responds "Well, after an intimate time here in bed, we could go for a walk, if you are up for it?"

"Yes, that sounds perfect, it will be lovely to get out in the fresh air" you respond.

"Excellent, let's start with this" he laughs as he pulls you in close and crashes his lips to yours as his hands begin to caress you from your face down to your most intimate area. You melt into his arms and caress every part of his body too, feeling each tight taut muscle ripple under your touch. You feel him harden

243

near your entrance and then penetrate you sending feelings of intense pleasure and passion rise through every extremity of your body. The rocking of your hips together makes you both moan with excitement and you both struggle for breath as you both reach the height of ecstasy. After laying next to each other your heart beats calm and your breath is regained enough to speak. "I love you so much Tori, I just cannot believe how lucky I am to have you as my wife" whispers Evan as he kisses the top of your head as he strokes your hair. You caress his chest and respond "Evan, you are everything to me, thank you agreeing to help me six months ago, I love you so much and cannot wait for what the future holds for us especially with our new little boy."

Evan pulls you in tighter and you both lay there together for a little while longer until your stomach starts to rumble. "Oh, someone is hungry by the sound of it" jokes Evan.

"Yes, baby boy is needing some breakfast this morning."

"Well let me get up and see what I can make for us" replies Evan as he attempts to climb out to the bed.

"Wait, I think you need one more of these before we get up" you laugh as you crash your lips to his.

"Oh, most definitely" says Evan as he reaches for his pants.

"Wait I will get up and help you" you say as you attempt to find your night gown.

"No, my darling wife, you stay there, I will go and make breakfast and be right back."

You smile sweetly at him as you flop back in the bed, pulling the covers up as you watch the birds playing in the tree outside.

A short time later, Evan reappears with muffins, a range of jams and two steaming cups of hot chocolate.

"Oh wow, where did this food come from, I just realised that we did not bring any with us" you ask as you take a muffin spread with strawberry jam and take a bite.

"Mum had the caretaker stock the cottage with all the supplies we would need for the next week."

"Oh, that is so thoughtful of her, wow these are delicious, try a bit" you say as you feed Evan a bit of your muffin.

"Mmm, yeah that is great" he replies, wiping crumbs from his lips.

After breakfast, you shower and dress for a day of exploring the cottage grounds and local township. The sun has dried the last of the morning dew and the flowers in the garden are stretched tall soaking up the late morning sun. In the distance you notice a herd of deer frolicking in the distance. They range in size from tiny littles babies to fully grown adults with impressive antlers. You just stop and watch them from a distance mesmerized by their elegant presence and free spirits enjoying the grass. After a while you and Evan continue your walk and you finally arrive at a picturesque watering hole. The water is crystal blue, and the scene reminds you of an oasis, with large trees lining the watering hole, as you and Evan get closer you notice the sight of fish majestically swimming close to the surface.

"This is my special place, I used to come here as a kid when we were on holidays, with my sketch pad and create my next dress design" says Evan as he reminisces.

"So, you have always wanted to be a fashion designer then?" you ask.

"Yes, I could not think of anything else, I loved the bright colours and different styles, Dad and Adam although surprised at my interest, luckily never made fun of me, they supported me every step of the way. And Mum, well she was beside herself with excitement, she loved fashion also as you can see by the cottage, she has a flair for design, she would often critique my work and offer the much-needed female perspective.

"Oh, that is wonderful, that your family was always so supportive of you. I don't really remember Mum and Dad that much, but Grandma was amazing as you know, she supported Jasper and I to reach for the stars and be anything we wanted to be."

"We both have been very lucky then" says Evan as he skims a pebble across the water narrowly missing a fish in its path. "Oh, sorry fisho, nearly got you" he replies shrugging his shoulders.

You spend some time sitting by the watering hole watching the fish swim around peacefully together and then decide to head back to the cottage and head into town to explore the attractions.

There are so many beautiful little privately owned stores, selling a wide range of trinkets and handmade crafts. Each shop takes your breath away, you could spend hours searching each shop and spend hundreds of dollars, however you try to control yourself until you reach a little baby shop down the end of the arcade. As you enter the shop, the lady behind the counter warmly greets you and noticing your baby bump congratulates you both. The shop is beautifully decorated and adorned with special handmade toys and clothing. Your eyes settle on the biggest teddy bear you have seen in your life; it is handmade out of the softest fluffiest blue material. It is sweetly dressed in a little tuxedo with black bow tie. "Oh, my goodness Evan look at this" you say as you rush over to it. Evan follows you, "Oh wow that is gorgeous isn't it?"

The sales lady joins you. "Oh, you have found Rupert the bear, he is very special, I made him myself from scratch and dressed him myself, a real labour of love" she says.

"You have done an amazing job, he is magnificent, can I ask is he for sale?" you ask.

"Yes, he is, due to the time involved in creating him, he is priced at $350".

"It is worth every cent" Evan replies, "so detailed and life like too."

Evan looks at your face and seeing how much you love it, "We will take it, it will have pride of place in our little boy's nursery for sure."

"Really Evan, we can have it?" you ask.

"Yes, definitely darling"

"Oh, that is wonderful, I am so glad that Rupert will be going to a loving home with your little boy" says the sales lady as she helps pull Rupert from his resting spot on the shelf. Evan pays for the bear and hands it to you. You snuggle into it tightly as you leave the store.

You and Evan have unexpectedly timed your honeymoon to coincide with the town's annual country fair. The next day you and Evan decide to visit the fair. As you join the end of the entry queue, you remember visiting country fairs as a young girl with your grandma. You remember all the side shows, rides and farm animals displays. You cannot wait to share this experience with your own son when he is older. You glance at Evan and can see he is excited for the fair also. "Are you excited too?" you ask.

Evan looks at you smiling, "For sure, I love country fairs, we used to come here on holidays at the same time as the fair each year. Adam and I loved the roller coaster ride and side shows."

You both reach the front of the queue, pay your entry fee and enter the fair and notice a sign ahead for the baby farm animal display. "Oh Evan, can we go there first please" you plead.

Laughing, Evan replies "Of course sweetheart, lead the way."

You reach the display and set eyes on the baby animals "Oh look at these little cuties."

The attendant looks at you "Would you like to come in, feed and have a cuddle of the baby animals?"

You look at Evan, he nods smiling, "Yes, can we?" you respond excitedly.

"For sure, follow me" says the attendant as he gestures for you to enter the display, "Now take a seat on these hay bales, relax and the animals will come over to you."

You do as instructed, and sure enough the baby goats and lambs come over and start nuzzling your hands, the attendant passes you a supply of food and the goats and lambs start eating from your hand. Soon an assortment of puppies, piglets, geese, lambs and goats surround you. The attendant asks for your phones and takes some photos so you can remember the visit. Before you know it your time in the display comes to an end and you have to farewell the animals to allow the next eagerly awaiting group to have their turn. You give all the animals one last pat, thank the attendant and leave the display. "That was so much fun, those animals were so cute" you say.

"Yes, it was great fun" says Evan as you both keep walking and come across a fairy floss stand. "Wow, I haven't had fairy floss since I was a kid" you say.

Evan heads over to the stand, orders a fair floss stick for each of you and returns to you "Here you go Darling."

"Thank you" you take a bite, and it dissolves instantly in your mouth. "Oh, that is so good."

Evan nods in agreement, you look at him and start laughing. Evan looks at you in bewilderment, "What are you laughing at?"

Still giggling, you respond, "You have fairy floss on your nose and cheeks, let me get that for you" you reach in and gently clean the fairy floss off his cheek with your tongue.

The next stop is Side Show Alley, you spot the Laughing Clowns stall and decide to try your luck. You take your time and deposit the balls carefully and watch them one by one land in the top two notches. After your last ball reaches its mark, the attendant comes and adds up your total "Congratulations Madam, you have reached our second highest score ever, you have your choice of anything on our prize rack." You scan the prizes and then decide on a large brightly coloured stuffed dog. As the attendant hands it to you they say, "Great choice, Congratulations." Evan raises his eyebrows, "Well played sweetheart."

You keep walking through the games and then reach a dart display. Evan stops to look closely at this. "Hey sweetheart, have a go at this one" you say encouragingly.

"Heck, why not" says Evan as he picks up the darts and starts sizing up his task. He needs to burst a series of slow-moving balloons with the darts. He gets ready to aim the dart, it hits its mark, he repeats the motion again and again until he has thrown all the darts. He has achieved a great result, only missing the mark once. The attendant responds, "Excellent job Sir, you can choose anything from the top row." Evan peruses the choices and makes his decision. "I will have that one 3rd from the left please." He has chosen a large teddy bear in a bridal dress with a bright red bouquet. As the attendant hands it to him, Evan then passes it to you, "For you, my bride."

You blush as you grab it with your free hand "Why thank you kind Sir."

Seeing your hands full with both toys, Evan takes the dog from you, and you continue your tour around the fair. Soon you reach the ride area. There is a large selection of rides to choose from, ranging from carousel rides, Ferris wheels, dodgem cars, haunted houses and roller coasters." You turn to Evan and ask, "Which ride do you want to go on?"

Evan thinks for a while and then responds, "I think we should go on the Ferris wheel."

"Good choice, Let's do it" you respond. You reach the head of the queue and make your way into the gondola; the attendant secures the door, and you begin to climb to the top. The views are amazing, you see the town centre and as you reach the top you are certain you can see your cottage in the distance. The ride lasts for four rotations and as you make you way to the bottom Evan kisses you. As you exit the ride you decide to return next year with baby boy. You continue through the fair checking out all the talented handmade crafts and cooking displays. "Wow, people are so talented, look at that patchwork quilt, it is beautiful" you say.

Evan nods in response, "Oh wow, look at that chocolate cake, look at the decorations, it looks almost too beautiful to eat" laughs Evan.

Your last stop on your way out of the fair is the Show Bag Pavilion, and both stock up on a wide variety of candy and chocolate and then the cool afternoon weather starts to set in and you both head back to the cottage for a romantic night in front of the fire.

The rest of your week long honeymoon is spent taking day trips exploring the countryside together and enjoying your time together before you return to reality and begin to prepare for baby boy's arrival.

CHAPTER 18

*T*he day arrives for you to return to the office after your magical honeymoon. On the drive into the office, you and Evan decide to have the difficult discussion about what to do with Rene, following the revelation that she spied on you both and reporting to Jasper. "So, what are we are going to do about Rene?" Evan asks.

"Well, even though things have worked out now with Jasper, I still feel very hurt by Rene's actions and do not feel that I can ever trust her again" you reply.

Evan nods in agreement, "If she has betrayed us once, she could very easily do it again."

You take a deep breath, "As much as it pains me to say, I think we will have to let her go, the risk is too great."

"Agreed, we should do it sooner rather than later, no need to prolong the inevitable" says Evan as you pull into the office carpark.

The elevator doors open, and cheers erupt from your colleagues who have all been anxiously awaiting your return. "Welcome back you two" yells Rene over the loud cheers and claps.

You and Evan are shocked but so appreciative of the fanfare for your arrival. "Thank you so much everyone, you did not have to do this really" says Evan as he pulls you in close beside him.

You respond, "This is amazing everyone, we love it thank you all so much."

You spend some time catching up with everyone and telling everyone about the wonderful week away you both had and before long it is time to get back into work. You open up your emails and your heart sinks at the number that have accumulated in such a short time. One by one you start sorting through them all and attending to what needs to be done.

The time has finally arrived for your chat with Rene, you have been avoiding it for as long as possible, Evan joins you in your office. "Darling, are you ready to have the chat with Rene?"

Reluctantly, you nod in response, then you call Rene into your office "Hi Rene, would you mind joining Evan and I in my office for a few minutes please?"

Rene nods her head and follows you into the office, you close the door behind you, "Take a seat Rene, we have something we need to discuss with you."

"Sure, no problem" replies Rene as she takes a seat.

You begin by saying "Rene, there is no easy way to ask this, but can you please tell me about your relationship with my brother Jasper?"

Rene sits upright in her seat, "What do you mean Tori?" she asks her voice shaking.

"Rene, I think you know what I mean, have you been in a relationship with my brother Jasper?"

Rene's face turns pale "How did you find out?, Did Jasper tell you?" she asks shortly.

"No, it was not Jasper, but a very trustworthy source provided clear evidence of your relationship with my brother."

"Alright Alright, Jasper and I have been in a relationship for several months now. We were in love; he told me he wanted to be with me" says Rene.

"I am not sure how significant your relationship is or was with Jasper, that is not my main concern right now. It has come to our attention, that you have been feeding important information about Evan and I, and the business to Jasper" you say firmly.

"No, that is not true, I have not" Rene tries to defend herself.

"There is no denying it Rene, we have received evidence that you have been in fact feeding information to Jasper" says Evan raising his voice.

"I don't believe you, what evidence do you have?" Rene asks smugly.

"We have evidence of text messages between you and Jasper going back several months, and video surveillance. Why would you betray us like that?" Evan asks angrily.

Rene sits in silence; she knows she has been caught out. "I am sorry Tori and Evan, Jasper approached me, and he was so sweet, and we started going out, and after a few dates he started to ask questions about you two and the business. I thought it was harmless, I had no idea he was going to use it against you, I am so sorry" Rene says as she begins to sob.

"Rene, we are so disappointed in you, you hold a very important position in this company. What you have done is disturbing and huge breach of our trust" you say firmly.

"I know, I am so sorry, Tori, please forgive me, Jasper has actually broken things off with me now" sobs Rene.

"We are sorry to hear that, but unfortunately the damage has been done. As I said you have

261

seriously breached our trust, we cannot trust you. I am sorry Rene, but due to the seriousness of this, we have no choice but to terminate your employment immediately" you say.

"No, please it will never happen again" begs Rene.

"I am sorry Rene, the decision has been made, you will need to leave immediately" says Evan.

Rene continues to sob, you feel for her, but you stand firm. "I will arrange for a good payout for you, but as Evan says you will need to leave immediately."

Rene wipes her face stands up and storms out of the office back to her desk to collect her belongings. Evan follows her to ensure she gets to her car safely. When he returns the emotions take over and you are in tears yourself. Although Rene's behaviour was unforgiveable, you did view her as a friend, and feel bad for her situation. Evan holds you close, "It's ok lovely, I know it's tough, but we did the right thing for the company."

You nod as you cry into his shoulder as he rubs your back. Once you compose yourself, you say to Evan, "We need to hold a staff meeting to tell them about Rene's departure."

"Of course, darling, but not right now, it can wait until the morning" replies Evan.

"No, it needs to be done now, I want everyone to be told straight away, I want them to hear our side first, in case Rene, contacts anyone before we get a chance to speak." you reply.

"Ok, good point, Are you sure you are up for this now? I can tell everyone if you prefer?" asks Evan.

"I am fine, I can do it. Can you round everyone up please?" you ask.

"Of course," Evan replies as he kisses you on the forehead and then heads out to round up the staff.

You enter the foyer where all the staff are gathered. "Hi everyone, sorry to drag you away from your duties, but we have an important announcement to make. I wanted you all to hear it straight away from us. Unfortunately, some information came to light to us recently regarding Rene, and unfortunately this information made it impossible for her to continue her employment with us. As such she has unfortunately left us immediately. It was a difficult but necessary decision, and we wish her all the best."

The crowd gasps and stare at each other in shock. Calvin finally speaks, "What happened?" he asks.

Evan replies, "Unfortunately Calvin, we are unable to disclose that information, it is between Rene and us."

"Oh ok" replies Calvin raising his eyebrows.

"Ok everyone, that is all I wanted to say for now, thank you again for listening, you can all return to your duties now" you say, and the crowd disperses.

At the end of the day, you arrive home to find Jasper waiting on your doorstep.

"Hey Jasper, what are you doing here?" you ask in surprise.

"Hi Tori and Evan, we need to talk."

"Ok come in" Evan gestures for Jasper to follow you inside.

Once settled in the lounge room, "I heard what you did to Rene, Why would you do that?" Jasper asks annoyed.

"Did Rene talk to you, I thought you were over?" you ask in response.

"Well, yes, we are no longer together, but she is still a friend, and I still care about her" replies Jasper.

"We found out that Rene had been feeding you information, she betrayed us, and the company and we could not trust her anymore, so we had to let her go" states Evan.

"But I feel responsible, she was only trying to help me" replies Jasper raising his voice.

"Yes, but at our expense and the expense of the company. That was unacceptable" replies Evan with a raised voice.

"Evan, Jasper, enough" you interrupt, "Jasper, the decision has been made, we could not trust Rene any longer and we had to let her go, it is sad yes, but we had to do what was right for the company."

After a short time, Jasper reluctantly replies, with arms raised in the air as though conceding defeat, "Alright, Alright I understand but I am not happy about it."

"Good, Ok, let's let this conversation end then" you say looking sternly at both Evan and Jasper.

They both concede defeat and nod in agreement with you.

"Good, now lets have a snack and talk about happier things shall we?" you say as you make your way to the kitchen to prepare drinks and afternoon tea.

Both Jasper and Evan join you in the kitchen, "So Jasper, have you given any more thought to taking an ownership share in the company as we discussed some time ago?" you ask as you hand Evan and Jasper a beer from the fridge.

"Well yes Tori I have, that is the main reason for my visit today, I have some news to share" he replies, his face lightening up.

"Oh really, by the look on your face, it is good news" you reply.

"Well, yes, it is really good news, I have been offered a lead in movie."

"Oh, that is great news" you respond excitedly as you make your way around the kitchen bench and pull Jasper in for a big hug. "I am so happy for you, tell us about it."

"Well, due to confidentiality, I can't say to much, but it is a romantic comedy, where two childhood sweethearts meet back up after many years apart and find their way back to each other. I would say that it probably isn't my usual film genre, but I was not going to pass up a lead, as it may lead to something else in the future," Jasper explains.

"Oh, that sounds great, I can't wait to see it, when do you start filming?" you ask.

"Well, filming will start in two weeks' time in LA, I have to head there next week to get settled."

"Oh, so soon, will you be back in time for the baby?" you ask concerned.

Jasper reaches for your hands, "Tori, I am sorry, filming will be at least six months minimum, but I promise to take a short break to fly back when you have the baby, I have already mentioned it to the producers and they are fine with it," Jasper squeezes your hands gently.

"Oh, ok, then well that is good to hear then, I wish you could be here for longer, but I am so excited for you" you reply as you hug Jasper tightly again.

"That is great news Jasper, good on you" says Evan as he reaches out to shake Jasper's hand.

"Yes, I am so excited about this" replies Jasper, "To finally get a movie lead is what I have been working for, for a long time. So, getting back to the ownership offer, I have thought about this and thank you for your kind offer, but I will say no. The fashion industry is not my forte, it is yours Tori, you and Evan are doing a fantastic job, you are fulfilling Grandma's legacy perfectly. I will not take it away from you. I apologise again for my behaviour over the last few months, I will back down, I will not contest Grandma's will. She made the right decision leaving the company to you."

"Oh, are you sure Jasper?" you ask.

"Yes definitely Tori, the company is yours, but I still would like my monthly profit distribution though" replies Jasper laughing.

"Of course, Bro, thank you for the kind words and the faith you have in Evan and I, it means so much to us both."

"Thanks Jasper, it is a relief for sure, and rest assured, Tori and I will definitely look after your Grandma's legacy, she was an inspiration to me and all her employees," says Evan as he give Jasper a hearty hug.

"Well, you two, what do you say we go out for dinner to celebrate tonight? My shout" asks Jasper excitedly.

"Well, if you are shouting big bro, then you are on" you reply quickly.

The three of you head out and enjoy a lovely evening talking about the business, Jasper's upcoming movie and plans for baby boy's arrival. At the end of the evening, you prepare to say goodbye to Jasper, and try to fight back tears. "Bro, I am so proud of you, you will rock this movie, I am sure, don't forget you little sister when you are a famous heart throb," you say as you playfully slap Jasper's shoulder.

"Thanks Tori, of course I will never forget you" he responds as he give you a big hug and wipes tears away from his eyes.

"Keep in touch Jasper, let us know when you get there next week," you reply.

"Congratulations again Jasper, can't wait to see you on the big screen" say Evan.

"Thanks, you look after my sister alright" says Jasper as he sternly waves a finger at Evan.

"For sure, do not worry about that" replies Evan as he places his arm around your shoulder pulling you in closely.

With that Jasper waves goodbye and heads to his car. You turn to Evan and tears begin to flow."Darling, it is alright, he will be back when our little boy comes" says Evan as he strokes your hair softly.

"I know, it is just that I just got him back, and now he is gone again."

"I understand" replies Evan as you watch Jasper drive away and turn to head inside.

CHAPTER 19

*T*he next two months fly by in a flash, Jasper has been keeping in touch regularly and thoroughly enjoying his new role. As promised, Jasper called off contesting the will, and he has removed the injunction on Blaze designs, so business is ramping up again with orders increasing with every day that passes. The orders from Lily's have increased the initial projected order which is spurring all the designers especially Evan to put in the extra effort required to create new hugely anticipated designs. You have spent the last month extensively training Amy your new assistant who is proving to be an invaluable asset to the business, and you have full faith that she will be able to fully handle things while you take some much-needed time off following the ever-impending birth of baby boy. The official due date is a little under three weeks away, but at the last appointment last week, he is already positioning himself ready for birth so he could make his arrival at any time. Evan is being so sweet and anxiously fussing and checking your every move, so much so that with the full uncomfortable way in which you are now feeling he is beginning to get on your nerves. You try to remain calm, but you cannot help but regretfully snap at his hovering sometimes.

As you sit in your office replying to emails and engrossed in checking sales figures, Evan comes in with some lunch. "Hey Darling, ready for a lunch break, I have your favourite, Ham and salad roll," he asks excitedly.

You loose your place in the spreadsheet and can't help but mutter a slow growl at his interruption. You look up him and try to smile, "Yes, Ok" you reply.

"Is everything ok, are you feeling alright?" Evan asks as he looks at you worriedly.

"I am fine, I was just working on the latest sales figures, and I lost my place," you reply slightly annoyed.

"Sorry, I thought we could have lunch together" he replies sheepishly.

"Of course, I am sorry, I am just a bit uncomfortable is all, I can't sleep properly and always need to use the bathroom" you reply.

"I know, you have been very restless lately, well the doctor says it shouldn't be too long now."

"I know I can't wait for him to be here" you reply as you make your way to the couch to join Evan, just as you sit down " Oh no" you say.

"What, what is it" asks Evan as he drops his lunch to jump up.

"I need to use the bathroom again" you say as you struggle to your feet.

Evan tries to hold back a giggle as he helps you to your feet. "It is not funny, don't laugh" you say as you waddle out of the office to the bathroom.

As you make your way back to the office, you gently rub your belly and softly say "Come on baby boy, please come soon, Mummy is so uncomfortable.

Baby boy gives a little kick as if mocking you. "It is not funny baby boy!" you say rubbing the area he just kicked.

You gently sit back down on the couch next to Evan who has been patiently waiting for you to return, he smiles at you and rubs your belly and gives you a kiss on the cheek. "You are doing an amazing job Tori; it will be so worth it."

You nod in response and begin to devour the lovely fresh roll that Evan bought for you.

After eating you sit in silence resting your head on Evan's chest next to you as he strokes your shoulder and hair. Before you know it, the poor sleep you had the night before and the fatigue of the final stages of the pregnancy catch up with you and you fall asleep in Evan's arms. An hour later, you wake up and are shocked to realise that you fell asleep in the office. As you sit up you notice that Evan has also been napping and he sleepily opens his eyes. You both look at each other in surprise. "Oh no, how long were we napping for?" you ask. Evan stretches and checks his watch, raises his eyebrows and replies "I reckon it was at least an hour I think."

You both look around the office and notice that someone has come in while you were both sleeping and cleared your lunch plates, gently placed a blanket over you both and quietly closed the door behind them to let you both rest. As you both shake off your nap, you both feel better and ready to get back to your work. Evan kisses you and heads back to his office; you hear him pass by Amy on the way. " Hi Evan, is Tori available for our next training session?" Amy asks.

"Yes, Amy she is ready waiting for you" he clears his throat "Thanks for looking out for us just now" whispers Evan as he nods to Amy .

"My pleasure Evan" replies Amy smiling as she gathers her notebook and makes her way to your office, she gently knocks on the door

"Hi Tori, are you ready to go through the Sales report again with me."

"Oh yes Amy of course, come in" you reply making sure you are presentable after your nap. "Amy, I must apologise for falling asleep just now, I haven't been able to sleep very well the last few weeks with the pregnancy etc."

Amy smiles in response, "Please Tori, don't apologise at all, I remember what I was like during the last few weeks of my pregnancy, it is amazing you are still able to be here at all." Amy has an 18-month-old little girl Sheila, and has been a wonderful support to you since joining the firm offering you advice and information on mother's groups etc.

You and Amy spend the rest of the afternoon, reconciling and summarising the recent sales figures and decide to head home.

As you arrive home, Evan runs you a warm bubble bath to help you relax while he prepares dinner for your both. As you lay back relaxing in the bath, you begin to feel a slight pain in your stomach. You sit upright in the bath and rub your stomach, "Oh baby what was that, is the water too warm for you?" you ask. The pain goes away and you relax again. Shortly after, Evan comes in to let you know that dinner will be ready soon. As you sit up to hop out of the bath, you feel another small pain that stops you in your tracks. "Ooh there is that pain again" you think to yourself as you begin to dry yourself and get dressed ready for dinner. By the time you reach the kitchen the pain is gone, and you sit down to enjoy your meal.

Later that evening as you and Evan are cuddled together on the couch the pain begins again, a little more intense than earlier, you cannot help but jump with a start and breathe deeply until the pain eases off. "Tori, darling are you ok?" Evan asks watching you intensely.

"I am not sure; I just got another sharp pain" you reply.

"What? What do you mean another sharp pain, have you had others? Why didn't you tell me?" asks Evan anxiously as he sits up straight and focuses on you.

"I had a couple earlier when I was having the bath, but then they stopped, so I didn't think anything of it, Oh no, it is starting again" you grimace as you reach for Evan's hand and squeeze it tightly as you wait a few seconds for the pain to stop.

"Tori, I think we should go to the hospital now and get you checked out" says Evan with a start as he jumps up and tries to help you up from the couch.

"No, No I will be fine, it has gone now, sit back down it has stopped now" you reply as you gesture for Evan to sit back down next to you.

"No Tori, I am not taking any chances, come on we are going to the hospital right now" as he races to the bedroom to grab the hospital bag you have put together.

When he returns he helps you up. "Evan I think you are overreacting; baby boy is not due yet"

"I don't care, the doctor said last week, he could come anytime now, I want to know you are ok come on" he says as he helps you to the door.

Just as you reach the door you feel another stabbing pain in your abdomen stopping you in your tracks as you double over. As you regain your breath, you say "Oh, maybe you are right, we should be doubly sure that everything is ok, that was a bit more intense than the others."

You and Evan make the short trip to the hospital and the pains are becoming more regular and each one just a bit more intense that the one before. A nurse welcomes you and quickly escorts you both to a birthing suite. "Sounds like we are going to have a baby tonight" she says as she helps you up on to the hospital bed. "A doctor will be in shortly to examine you" she says as she leaves both you and Evan alone in the room.

"Hey Darling, looks like our baby boy wants to meet us a bit earlier than planned" says

Evan as he caresses your forehead as you begin to have another contraction.

Just as the contraction ends, your doctor appears in the room "Hi Tori and Evan, lets see how long before baby boy arrives shall we"?

The doctor begins to examine you, "Well I can confirm you are definitely in labour Tori, but it may be a while before he arrives, you still have a way to go before you are fully dilated. Just try to relax as much as you can."

"Easier said than done Doctor" you snap in reply.

"Everything is going smoothly, your waters are yet to break, once they do I suspect things will move along with a bit more speed. I will be back to check on you soon, the nurse will be just outside, press the buzzer if you need anything at all" says the doctor as she heads out of the room.

You spend the next five hours having contractions before your waters eventually break. The doctor comes back in, reexamines you again, "Good news Tori, you are fully dilated now, it is go time, let's meet this little man" says the doctor excitedly as she gathers all the nursing staff to assist.

Evan kisses you on the forehead, "It is nearly over, you have got this, our son will be here soon."

You nod in response just as another intense contraction begins, you scream out and squeeze Evan's hand so tightly, you see it turn white in colour. Evan grimaces slightly but focuses intently on you encouraging you to keep going.

"Ok Tori, I can see the head now, with the next contraction I need you to push with everything you have Ok" encourages the doctor.

You nod in response and seconds later you feel the contraction begin, you focus all your strength and push with everything you have "Good Darling, that's it, he is coming, you are doing brilliantly" encourages Evan.

"Yes Tori, I reckon one more good push should do it, are you ready?" says the doctor.

Before you can respond the contraction begins and again you push with everything you have.

"Excellent Tori, you have done it, your son is out, congratulations he is perfect" says the doctor.

Evan looks at his son and then at you with tears in his eyes, "You did it Darling, he is here, and he is gorgeous, I love you so much" and he kisses you deeply."

"Evan do you want to cut the cord?" asks the doctor.

Speechless Evan nods and takes the scissors from the doctor and listens to the instructions and makes the cut and then your son is placed on your chest.

The events of the last few hours come crashing down and you begin to sob as you hold and caress your baby boy.

The nurses allow you to bond for a few moments and then takes your son away to clean him up and do all the necessary checks required. They turn to you both smiling, "Congratulations to both of you, your son is perfect, we will get you settled in a ward, and we will bring him back to you both shortly."

Still crying, you watch him as you are wheeled out of the delivery room and taken to a hospital room. Evan does not leave your side.

Shortly after the nurses reappear with your son, Evan eagerly reaches for him, and you watch him smile widely as he holds his son in his arms. Evan comes and sits on the bed next to you. "Thank you Darling, he is perfect" he says not taking his eyes of his new son.

"Yes he is pretty special isn't he" you reply as you take in the sight of your new son.

The three of you bond together for the next few hours until you can no longer fight the urge to sleep, baby boy rests in Evan's arms and you take the opportunity to catch some sleep.

The next morning when you wake up, Evan is still there watching baby boy intently in his crib.

"Good morning sweetheart how are you feeling?" he asks.

"A little sore but good, how is he?" you ask.

"He is perfect, Hey, are you up for couple of visitors? Mum and Dad have just arrived and are waiting outside?"

"Of course, help me clean myself up a bit and then let them in" you respond, excited to show off your new son.

Minutes later, the door opens and Vivian and Xavier rush in excitedly holding a large blue teddy bear, flowers and congratulatory balloons."Oh, Tori darling, how are you?" says Vivian as she engulfs you with a huge hug and kiss.

"Hi Vivian, I am a bit sore and tired but so excited."

Vivian nods and then turns her attention to the small crib by the bed, "Oh my gosh, there here is" she exclaims as she rushes over and scoops him up, kissing his little head.

Xavier congratulates you and Evan also and joins his wife to meet his new grandson, you notice tears welling in Xavier's eyes as he fixates on the new baby. "He is perfect" he says as he reaches to hold the baby's tiny little hand.

Vivian still looking at the baby asks, " Does this little treasure have a name yet?"

You and Evan look at each other smiling and then you respond, "Yes, we have decided to name him after my late father Blake William McIntyre-Thomas."

"Oh, that is beautiful, welcome to the family Blake" coos Vivian.

The proud grandparents stay for a little while longer and then reluctantly leave to allow the three of you to bond some more and rest.

CHAPTER 20

*A*fter a short stay in hospital, the time arrives for you to take your baby boy home, you gently place him in his baby seat and Evan carefully drives his new family home. Once home you carry Blake inside "Hey Darling boy, this is your new home" you say as you make your way to the nursery. Blake gurgles in response and gently closes his eyes as you lay him in his crib for a nap. Evan joins you as you both watch him drift off to sleep, you both quietly sneak out of the nursery and make your way to the lounge. "Well, our baby boy is finally home" says Evan as he pulls you in close and kisses you on the forehead.

You nod in response, "Yes life will be very different now, I am sure" you say taking a deep breath as you rest your head on Evan's chest.

"Do you need anything?" asks Evan.

"No, I have everything I need right here, I just want to stay here and snuggle with you for a while."

"No problem my love, you rest up" says Evan as he squeezes you tightly.

Within minutes you drift off to sleep in Evan's embrace. A little while later you are awoken by baby Blake crying from the nursery.

"Stay there my love, I will go and get him and bring him out" says Evan.

"Thanks, he is probably hungry."

Evan returns with baby Blake, and you prepare to breast feed him, luckily he latches on quickly and has a good feed, you burb him and then pass him to Evan for cuddles. Your face lights up as you watch him gently rock Blake back and forth. "You are a natural with him" you say.

"Thanks darling" replies Evan smiling widely.

The time comes to retire for the evening, and you give Blake his last feed for the night, change his nappy and tuck him tightly into his crib which Evan moved into your room so as to be close to him should he stir in the night. Blake closes his little eyes and drifts off to sleep, you and Evan take the opportunity to climb into bed yourselves and get some much-needed rest before he wakes again. Evan cuddles up closely behind you, "Goodnight Darling, I am so happy to have my family home now" Evans whispers as he kisses your neck. You turn to face him and kiss him deeply, "I am so glad to be home too, goodnight sweetheart" and within minutes you both join Blake sleeping soundly.

Just an hour later, you both a jolted awake by Blake's cries. Evan jumps out of bed and rushes to the crib, "Hey Buddy, what is happening?" he asks as he gently picks up his son trying to soothe his cries.

Rubbing your eyes, you climb out of bed and join Evan, "He is not yet due for another feed just yet, maybe he needs a nappy change?"

"You go back to bed darling, let me take care of him" Evan says.

"Are you sure you don't need a hand?" you ask.

"No, us boys have this handled don't we buddy?" coos Evan as he heads to the nursery to check his nappy.

"Thank you Darling" you respond as you climb back into bed, pulling up the bed covers.

Minutes later, Evan and a settled Blake return, Evan carefully places his son back in the crib, kisses him gently and joins you back in the bed.

"How did you go?" you whisper eagerly.

"Great, he just needed a new nappy, all sorted, and he almost fell back to sleep by the time we got back in here" whispers Evan.

"Thank you, you are a wonderful father Darling."

Evan smiles, kisses you and pulls you in tightly towards him, and you all drift off to sleep.

The rest of the night passes by easily, Blake only woke a couple of times ready for his next feed.

The next morning your phone rings, waking you from your sleep, you are excited to see Jasper's number flashing on your phone.

"Good morning Jasper, How are you?" you ask excitedly.

"I am doing really well, but more importantly how are you and my nephew doing? I know you came home yesterday" Jasper replies.

"Yes, all is good" you yawn in response.

"I am sorry to wake you, I was at a cast dinner last night so I couldn't check in with you last night."

"That is fine, Blake is settling in, he woke a few times over night, but he is sleeping well now."

"Oh, that is great news, How is Evan coping?" Jasper asks with a laugh.

"He is wonderful, and so excited, he helped out overnight, and I hear him in the kitchen making us breakfast."

"That is great, well I will let you go, have to get ready for a filming session this morning, send me some pictures of my little nephew, I hope to get back to visit you in a couple of weeks when we are able to take a small break."

"That will be great Jasper, Blake will love to meet his Uncle J" you reply.

You finish the call and make your way to the kitchen after checking Blake is still sleeping soundly.

Evan smiles as you enter the kitchen, he looks tired after the broken sleep last night, "Good morning darling, breakfast is nearly ready" he says as he gestures for you to sit at the kitchen bench.

"You are up early, breakfast smells fantastic" you say as you give him a kiss as you take your seat at the bench.

"Yes, I couldn't get back to sleep after Blake needed his last nappy change, so I decided to get up and cook breakfast" he says as he starts serving your pancakes, eggs and bacon, "Was that Jasper on the phone?"

"Yes, he rang to check how we were settling in since coming home yesterday, he is planning a visit in a couple of weeks when there is a break in filming" you reply.

"Oh, that will be great" replies Evan as he settles down next to you and begins to eat breakfast.

Just as you take your last bite, Blake begins to cry, "Oh baby boy is ready for his breakfast" you laugh as you head to the crib and get ready for Blakes feeding session.

The rest of the day is spent sleeping, feeding and cuddling baby Blake.

The following few weeks fly by, and Blake is settling in well and growing bigger every day. As you are sitting in the lounge after just placing Blake down for his mid-morning nap, there is a knock at the door. Evan jumps up, "I will get it."

As he opens the door, Dean is standing there with a huge teddy bear and flowers.

"Hi Evan, Congratulations on the arrival of little baby Blake" says Dean with a huge smile.

"Hi Dean, how are you? Great to see you, come in, we were not expecting you."

"Yes, I was in the area visiting another client and I thought I would take the chance to drop in, hope I haven't come at a bad time?" he asks.

"Not at all Dean, come in, so glad you could drop in" you reply giving him a kiss on the cheek as he enters the living room. "Oh, thank you Dean, these are beautiful" you say as you take the bear and flowers from Dean.

As Dean settles on the couch, he opens his briefcase, "There is actually another reason, I dropped by" he says as he pulls out a large envelope. " Now that Blake is finally here,

294

Tori, you have now satisfied your late Grandmother's requirement of producing an heir, I have the paperwork here to formalise the transfer of McIntyre designs to you," he passes the paperwork to you.

You take the paperwork, and your hands are shaking, knowing your dream will soon be a reality. "Oh wow, thank you Dean" you say as you read the contracts.

"Jasper has signed his section and now all that is needed is for you to sign the contract and McIntyre designs will now be yours" states Dean as he points out where you are required to sign and hands you the pen. Without hesitation you take the pen and sign the appropriate sections, Evan pulls you in for a hug and kiss, "We did it babe, the company is yours."

"No darling, the company is ours, I asked Dean after Blake was born if he could change the contract to transfer ownership to both of us" you say.

"Oh, really you did that?" Evan asks in shock.

"Yes darling, this would not have happened without you, and you are an important part of this company, you deserve your share."

"Oh, Tori, thank you so much, you really didn't have to do that" replies Evan, tears forming in his eyes.

"Yes Evan, Tori was very adamant that she wanted you to have an equal share in this company" confirms Dean.

"And Jasper knows about this? And is Ok with this?"

"Of course Darling, I spoke to him at length about this, and he is in full agreement, as he said to us some time ago, he has no interest in running this company, and he knows that you and I will do what is best for McIntyre fashions, he is an actor, not a business man, as long as he continues to get his monthly profit distribution, he is more than happy to have us run the business" you reply reassuringly.

Evan thinks for a moment and then his face lights up as he pulls you in for tight embrace and kisses you deeply. "Tori, I cannot believe this, you have changed my life so much, a year ago I was just a single man struggling to fulfill my dreams of being a fashion designer and now, I am a husband, a father, have my own fashion label and now co-own a magnificent company with the woman of my dreams."

Dean clears his throat "Well, you have to sign this contract first, before your ownership is formalised" Dean jokes with a giggle.

"Oh of course, where do I sign?" asks Evan composing himself as he focuses on the task at hand as he prepares to sign the contract.

Once the papers are fully signed and witnessed by Dean, you all share a celebratory drink. As if on cue, Blake stirs from his sleep. You bring him out so that Dean can see him.

"Oh Tori, he is gorgeous, your grandmother would be so proud of you" says Dean as he gently strokes Blakes little hand.

"Oh, I hope so, I am sure she is watching over us" you reply.

"Yes for sure she is" says Dean, "Well I am so happy to have bought you this great news and met this beautiful little boy, but I must get going and get this papers lodged and make everything official. Congratulations you two, I mean three" Dean jokes as he gathers his belongings and heads out.

As Evan returns from seeing Dean off, he comes back into the room and cannot hold his smile as he pulls you and Blake in close to him tightly. "I mean it Tori, I am the happiest man alive right now, thank you so much."

"My pleasure my darling" you respond as you crash your lips on to his.

CHAPTER 21

A year has passed, McIntyre designs is growing in strength, you and Evan have worked tirelessly to build the business, secure more distributors and make McIntyre Designs a well-known highly sought after brand. The design team has doubled in size to keep up with demand and everyone is working like a well-oiled machine. You and Evan are so proud of what you have been able to achieve since taking over full ownership and continue to have plans to grow into the future as you investigate international markets also.

The time has arrived for Blake's first birthday party. Vivian has worked diligently to prepare for the big day, taking care of all the food, decorations and guest lists. You are so excited to see the endless balloons and streamers surrounding the walls of your home and the marquee outside. The air is filled with the aromas of finger food and cakes cooking.

"Vivian you have done an amazing job setting all this up, this is fantastic, thank you so much" you say as you give Vivian a hug.

"My pleasure sweetie is not every day my special little grandson turns one" smiles Vivian, "Besides Paige has helped me out enormously."

Paige turns around from preparing a platter, her large baby bump showing proudly, Adam and Paige are eagerly awaiting the arrival of the second child in just over a months' time. "I have been so excited to help out with this party Tori" says Paige smiling as she heads towards you for a big hug and kiss.

"Well thank you to both of you, I could not have done this with out you both, the guests should be arriving soon" you reply and as if on cue the doorbell sounds, and Lexie is excitedly standing on the other side with an armful of presents and supplies for the party.

"Hey Lexie, so excited to see you, come in" you say as you practically drag her inside. "Come into the kitchen, Vivian and Paige are there putting finishing touches on the food and decorations."

The ladies excitedly hug each other, and Lexie helps out with the rest of the streamers and table settings.

Once all the guests have arrived, it is time for the guest of honour to make his appearance. You dress Blake in dress pants and matching shirt and carry him out to the excited guests.

The guests cheer with excitement, Blake flinches in your arms at the noise, but then his face lights up with a smile and he excitedly begins to clap his little hands. He then reaches out for a nearby balloon with a brightly coloured streamer, the crowd continue to cheer for him and one by one come to him wishing him a happy birthday and kissing him.

The party is a success and Blake has generously received lots of gifts of toys, books and clothing. The time comes for the party to end and after farewelling your guests and cleaning up, Blake is sound asleep, and you and Evan decide to cuddle up together on the couch and discuss the events of the day. "Wow, that was a great day" says Evan.

"It sure was, everyone was so generous, our little boy had a great day, his little face didn't stop smiling the whole time" you reply.

"Yes, he did so well with all the excitement going on" says Evan.

"He is so tired, he is sound asleep now, don't think we will hear much out of him for a few hours" you reply laughing.

"Oh really, well I can think of something we can do to pass the time until he wakes up again" replies Evan cheekily as he crashes his lips to yours.

Understanding what he has in mind you deepen the kiss, rubbing your hands through his hair and up and down his back. Still with his lips on yours Evan gets up of the couch and lifts you in his arms and carries you to the bedroom and places you in the middle of the bed as he gently lowers himself on to you. You feel him begin to harden against his pants as you lift his shirt up to expose his strong muscular chest rubbing and squeezes his muscles. He softly moans as you continue to excite him. He reaches under your top and his hands make his way up to your breasts where he begins to caress and gently pinch your nipples, filling your body with excitement.

Minutes later you are both naked and caressing every inch of each other's bodies, kissing each other passionately as your tongues intertwine. The heat between you rise and you soon feel his hardness at your entrance. You open your legs and allow him to enter filling you entirely. You both begin to rock together in unison, the heat between you becoming more intense with each thrust of your hips. Evan groans as he releases inside you, filling you with his manhood. You both lay together regaining your breath and gently caressing each other as you both come down from your emotional and physical high.

With Blake still asleep, the events of the day catch up with you both and before you realise it you both fall asleep in each other's arms.

Several weeks later, you and Evan decide to take a family holiday to the beachside, you both excitedly look forward to sharing the beach with Blake, he has just began to find his feet and you can't wait to watch him paddle in the shallow water of the beach. The weather is warming up and it is going to be a beautiful late spring day. As you drive to your destination, Blake is excited in the back seat as you point out the scenery along the way. After arriving and checking in you decide to take a late afternoon stroll along the beach. The weather is still warm and is perfect for paddling along the water's edge. Evan and you walk along with Blake between you as the waves come crashing in and slowly make their way along the shoreline. As the water reaches Blake's feet he squeals with excitement as he watches the water dissipate. You spend time together building a sandcastle and then decide to head back to your accommodation for dinner.

You settle Blake down for the evening and then join Evan at the dining table for your meals, you have been able to order a special room service meal. As you both enjoy your roast meals and dessert you turn to Evan " Darling I have something I need to discuss with you."

Evan takes a sip of his drink and looks at you "Sure what do you want to talk about?" he asks.

You both focus on each other and you reach for Evan's hand. "Darling you are going to be a Dad again, I am pregnant."

Evan's eyes widen as he looks at you as he processes what you have just said and then his face breaks into a smile "Really are you sure?" he asks.

"Yes, I found out yesterday, but wanted to wait until we were here to tell you."

Evan jumps from his seat and rushes to you, picking you up in his arms and swirling you around as he kisses you.

As he regains himself he asks you "How far along are you? Are you feeling Ok?"

"Yes, I am feeling really good, the doctor thinks I am about 8 weeks along now" you reply smiling "So are you happy?"

"Oh yes Tori, I am so so happy, we are going to have another baby, this is fantastic" he replies and then his lips meet yours as he squeezes you tightly. "I didn't think I could be any happier than I was having you, Blake and the business, but you have just increased my happiness ten-fold. This is the best news ever; It would be perfect if we have a little girl this time around, it would make our family complete."

www.ingramcontent.com/pod-product-compliance
Lightning Source LLC
Chambersburg PA
CBHW070109120726
47909CB00002B/548